Praise for
THE BELLWOODS GAME

An ABA Kids' Indie Next List Pick
A Top 10 Indigo Best Kids' Book of The Year
An Indigo Kids Staff Pick
A Junior Library Guild Selection

"Krampien's eerie story cleverly focuses on themes such as
bullying. . . . This supernatural tale will chill readers while
reminding them that real friendship can brave any situation."
—*Booklist*

"Krampien intersperses atmospherically eerie black-and-white
art throughout a tense friendship novel steeped in local lore."
—*Publishers Weekly*

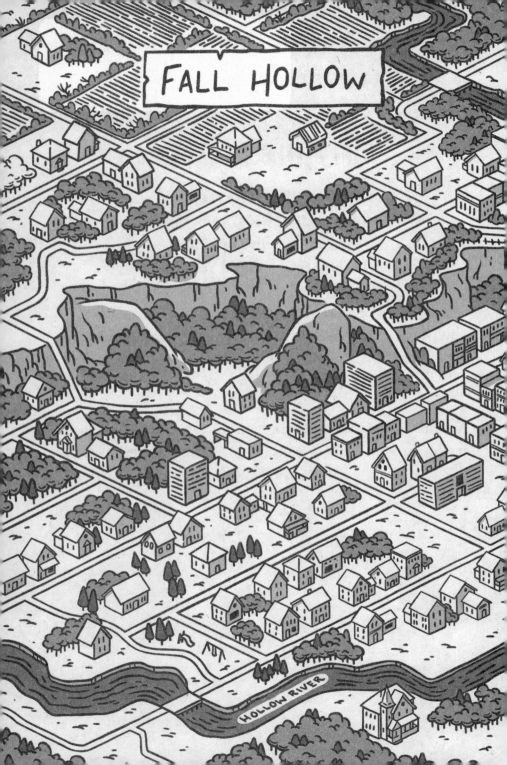

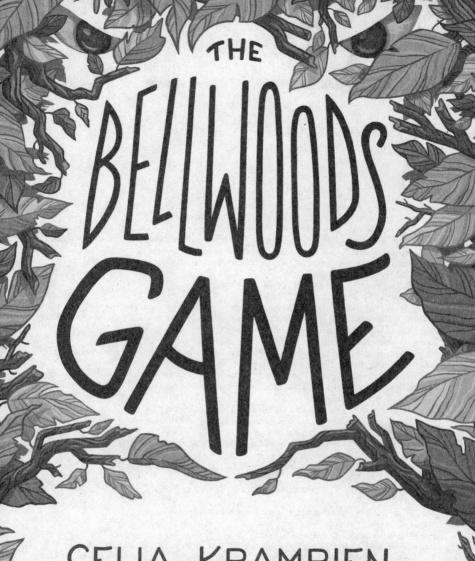

THE
BELLWOODS
GAME

CELIA KRAMPIEN

atheneum

Atheneum Books for Young Readers

New York   London   Toronto   Sydney   New Delhi

ATHENEUM BOOKS FOR YOUNG READERS
An imprint of Simon & Schuster Children's Publishing Division
1230 Avenue of the Americas, New York, New York 10020

Simon & Schuster: Celebrating 100 Years of Publishing in 2024
For information about special discounts for bulk purchases, please contact Simon & Schuster Special Sales at 1-866-506-1949 or business@simonandschuster.com.
The Simon & Schuster Speakers Bureau can bring authors to your live event. For more information or to book an event, contact the Simon & Schuster Speakers Bureau at 1-866-248-3049 or visit our website at www.simonspeakers.com.
Also available in an Atheneum Books for Young Readers hardcover edition
Interior design by Celia Krampen, Lauren Rille, and Jacquelynne Hudson-Underwood
The text for this book was set in Birka Lt. Pro.
The illustrations for this book were rendered digitally using Adobe Photoshop, a Wacom Cintiq, and an Apple iPad Pro.
Manufactured in the United States of America
0624 MTN
First Atheneum Books for Young Readers paperback edition July 2024
10 9 8 7 6 5 4 3 2 1
The Library of Congress has cataloged the hardcover edition as follows:
Names: Krampien, Celia, 1988- author, illustrator.
Title: The Bellwoods Game / Celia Krampien.
Description: First edition. | New York : Atheneum Books for Young Readers, [2023] | Audience: Ages 8-12. | Audience: Grades 3-7. | Summary: A group of sixth graders participating in an annual Halloween tradition to pacify the ghost of Abigail Snook quickly realize that the Bellwoods contains an even bigger threat to their town.
Identifiers: LCCN 2022014340 | ISBN 9781665912501 (hardcover) | ISBN 9781665912518 (paperback) | ISBN 9781665912525 (ebook)
Subjects: CYAC: Ghosts—Fiction. | Fear—Fiction. | Games—Fiction. | Friendship—Fiction. | Forests and forestry—Fiction. | Halloween—Fiction. | LCGFT: Thrillers (Fiction) | Novels.
Classification: LCC PZ7.1.K697 Be 2023 | DDC [Fic]—dc23
LC record available at https://lccn.loc.gov/2022014340

This one is for Andrea Morrison.
Thank you for believing in this story.

THE BELLWOODS GAME

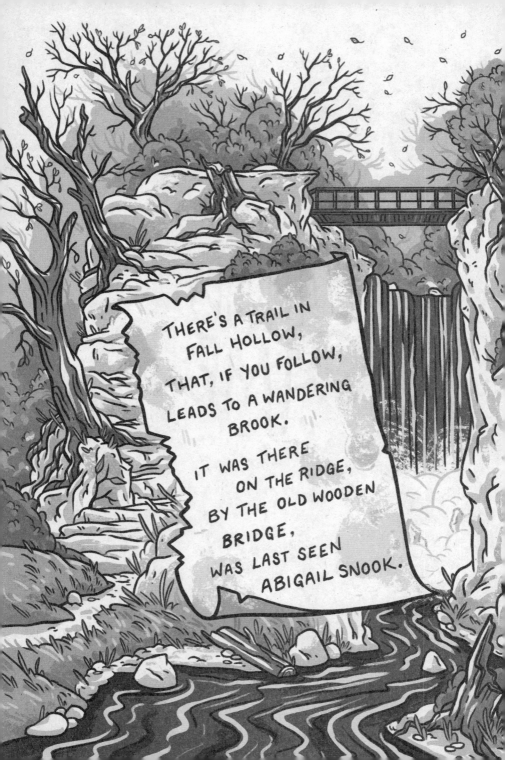

PROLOGUE
HALLOWEEN, SOME TIME AGO

Abigail didn't believe the stories about the woods.

Sometimes the kids at school pretended they were haunted. Was it the jack-o'-lanterns winking from porch steps that had reminded them of the old game? Or was it the woods dressed up in red and gold? More likely, they had grown tired of their usual methods of torment. After all, the game had to be more fun than knocking books out of Abigail's hands or flinging pencils at her in class.

"Nice costume, Abby. You off to Grandma's house in that getup?" Margery Danes said, eyeing the girl's red cloak when they crossed paths in the hall. She knocked into Abigail with a thrust of her bony shoulder as she passed. "Why don't we chat about it later? After school. I want to play a game with you."

Margery Danes wasn't the biggest sixth grader, but she was mean, and an invitation to chat was enough to make any kid's blood run cold. Because Margery always wanted more than a chat: lunch money, answers to tomorrow's math quiz, or those new sunglasses she was sure would look better on her. Abigail didn't know what Margery wanted today, but one way or another, she always got what she wanted.

Abigail lingered by her locker after the final bell. She watched other Beckett Elementary students hurry down the hall toward the front door, disguised as bedsheet ghosts, plastic pitchfork devils, and big-wigged pop stars. They talked of candy and trick-or-treating routes, confident any frights they'd encounter this evening would be of their own devising.

Abigail envied them.

Voices faded. The last of the stragglers trickled out into the thin autumn light. An eerie silence particular to empty schools pressed in close. Instead of heading for the door, Abigail tiptoed up a flight of stairs and paused on the landing, halfway between floors. She peered out a window where the whole schoolyard lay before her. A pinecone rattled around the empty basketball court, and the brisk wind whistled through the metal climbing bars. Nearby, Margery and her only friends, Jess Martin and Josie Spooner, leaned against a bike rack. They threw food, undoubtedly stolen from some kid's lunch earlier that day, onto the road for passing vehicles to crush. They laughed and cheered as an apple exploded beneath the wheels of a green pickup truck.

Abigail reached for the silver locket around her neck. She held it tight, feeling it grow warm against her palm. It had belonged to her grandmother who had passed away last summer. Whenever Abigail felt worried, she held her locket and remembered her grandmother's strong hugs and gentle smile. But no matter how hard she gripped it today, Abigail's worries remained. So did Margery, Josie, and Jess. They lounged against the bike rack, shooting glances toward the school, keeping watch for their prey.

Abigail sighed, pulled a book from her backpack, and made herself small beneath the window.

She would have to wait them out.

She waited three chapters' worth. Then she waited some more. Finally, when the light in the stairwell had grown dim, she dared another peek out the window.

3

Crisp leaves skittered across the deserted schoolyard. Clouds the color of a day-old bruise hung heavy in the sky. Even from inside, Abigail could smell the threat of rain.

She tucked her book away, slung her bag over her shoulder, and hurried down the stairs. The school doors banged shut behind her as the first rumble of thunder rolled overhead.

There was no sign of Margery or anyone else as Abigail crossed the junior soccer field, making for the Bellwoods forest. The woods hugged the schoolyard in a choking embrace, and tall pines lined the edges like silent sentinels. There was a small break in the tree line where a well-trod path lay, one Abigail took every day to and from school. She stepped into the woods just as thunder crashed loud above the treetops, drowning out another sound—the clang of a bell.

Abigail's footsteps crunched as she rushed down the narrow path made of dirt and stones. Exposed roots snaked across the surface, and leaves collected at the edges in the tall grass.

Ahead, the path twisted out of sight and into darkness. If she hurried, she'd make it home before getting caught by the storm. Or anyone else, she hoped.

Then she heard a ghoulish wail.

It was a small sound at first. Soon, two more spine-chilling cries joined. The cacophony rose to a howling shriek, then faded and died. Familiar snickers of laughter followed.

A knot of dread pulled tight in Abigail's stomach. She quickened her pace but refused to run. That's what they wanted, wasn't it? They craved the chase. They wanted her fear, but she wouldn't give it to them. Not today.

Thunder barked, closer this time. Wind whistled through the treetops like a chorus of calling spirits. Then another ghostly wail floated out of the gloom, followed by more cold laughter.

"Abby!" came Margery's voice, muffled by the thickness of the wood. "A spirit is after you. These woods are haunted, don't you know?"

"Go away!" She couldn't see them, not yet. But she could hear the rustle of bodies moving in the shadows and feel their watchful eyes on her.

"C'mon, don't you want to play the game, Abby?" Margery again. "You know the one. If you can beat us to the old bell, I'll give you something special—a gift. But if you don't, then you owe *me* something instead. Just like we used to play."

Abigail groaned. She knew the game. Everyone at Beckett did. Kids pretended to be ghosts who chased the other players while they ran for the old bell that sat deep in the forest. Those who reached the bell were home free. But players who got caught? They became ghosts too. Unless they had something to sacrifice, of course.

"Do we have a deal?" The words hung in the air like a threat.

Abigail didn't wait to hear more. She forgot her earlier

promise to herself and flew down the path, her cloak billowing and leaves flying up behind her like startled birds. Because it didn't matter what Abigail said. The game had already begun.

She dodged potholes and leaped over the fallen trees crowding the path. Long tangles of grass reached for her like grasping hands, but she didn't slow down, not even as more ghoulish cries erupted behind her.

Soon, the sound of rushing water met her ears. The Hollow River came into view. It was inky black in the gloom, cutting through the landscape like a deep gash. The path veered left to follow the river, and together they snaked through the woods and out of sight. Abigail followed.

The path brought her to the base of a steep slope where, high above, sat a rocky ridge. Tree roots, exposed by countless climbing feet, made a sort of staircase. Abigail scrambled up while, overhead, thunder continued to roll.

"Aaaaabigail!" It was Josie this time, voice high and taunting.

"The ghosts are going to get you. Soon you'll be a ghost too!" cried Jess, breathless from the chase.

Abigail's feet slipped, sending dirt and stones cascading in her wake. She grabbed hold of a nearby tree for support.

Then she felt a hand on her ankle. It yanked—hard. Abigail fell to her hands and knees. Sharp rocks scraped her palms and tore at her jeans as Margery pulled her down the slope.

"I got her! That's it, you lose!" cried Margery, voice shrill with victory.

Abigail's hands clawed at the earth, searching, scrabbling, frantic.

"You know the rules. Cough up your loot," said Margery.

"I don't have anything for you," said Abigail through gritted teeth. She struggled against Margery's grasp.

"Yes, you do." Margery tugged on Abigail's foot, dragging her farther down the slope. Abigail twisted onto her back. She saw Margery eye her grandmother's locket.

"No!" Abigail squirmed.

"C'mon, Abby. Those are the rules of the game. Unless you want to join the ghosts, you gotta sacrifice something." Margery reached for the locket.

At that moment, Abigail felt the hand around her ankle loosen.

She kicked.

Her foot caught Margery in the shoulder. The girl tumbled backward, landing with a heavy thud at the base of the slope. There was an angry outburst from Jess and Josie, but Abigail didn't care. She found her feet and scrambled up the slope.

The trees were sparse on top of the ridge, offering thin protection against the gathering storm. Wind whipped Abigail's face and tugged at her braid. There was a sudden flash and a crash of thunder. Abigail reeled back and stumbled. Wild-eyed, she peered to her right where the forest floor gave way to a steep drop-off. Far below, the Hollow River churned. Crisp leaves swirled on its surface, then disappeared, down into the river's cold, dark depths. Another crash shook the sky. Rain-drops dotted Abigail's cheeks.

She sprinted toward home, following the winding path along the rocky ridge. The roar of rushing water filled her ears. Finally, an old wooden bridge came into view, spanning Fall Hollow's most scenic lookout, Silver Falls. Abigail caught glimpses of it through the trees as she ran, water cascading over a rocky ledge, then falling several stories to meet the churning Hollow River below. It was a beautiful sight, but the students of Beckett Elementary were often more concerned with what lay beyond—the old bell.

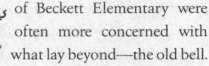

The bell that gave the woods its name was large and rusted and perched atop a pile of stones. It sat in a broad clearing just on the other side of the bridge. Reaching the bell usually marked the end of the game for Beckett students. But it wouldn't today.

"You made me rip my jeans!" cried Margery, voice carrying on the wind. "But at least I got what I came for."

Abigail stopped. Her hand

went to her collarbone where her locket should have been. But her fingers found nothing. Her locket was gone, snatched away during the scuffle.

She should have kept running. But thinking about her grandmother's locket around Margery's neck, Abigail felt anger swell inside of her so fierce, it swallowed her usual fear whole. Her fingers curled into tight, trembling fists. She turned and marched back to the ridge.

Down below, Margery showed off her prize to Jess and Josie. Abigail's locket glinted in the low light.

They looked small then, Abigail thought. Just three mean kids with nothing better to do than play pretend in the woods, using an old game as an excuse to take what didn't belong to them. This, Abigail decided, ended today. She wasn't going to play their game anymore.

At that moment, a blinding flash lit the woods. An ear-splitting CRACK followed, and rain poured down hard and swift like the river spilling over at Silver Falls.

The last thing Margery, Jess, and Josie saw was Abigail on top of the ridge. Illuminated by the lightning, her face looked as pale as a ghost's. The eyes beneath her furrowed brow were dark, unseeing pools. Her hair, set loose by the wind, swirled around her head as if possessed.

All three recoiled at the sight. They bolted down the path, back the way they had come. Not one of them looked back.

They didn't see Abigail stumble.

They didn't see her feet slide over the rain-slick rocks, then find nothing but air.

All they had done was play a game in the woods. When Margery, Jess, and Josie saw her last, Abigail was fine. Just fine. And that's what they told the police the next morning.

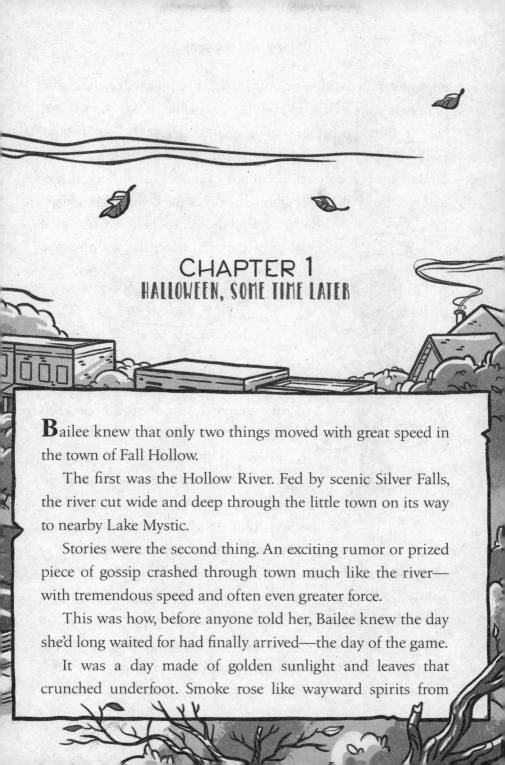

CHAPTER 1
HALLOWEEN, SOME TIME LATER

Bailee knew that only two things moved with great speed in the town of Fall Hollow.

The first was the Hollow River. Fed by scenic Silver Falls, the river cut wide and deep through the little town on its way to nearby Lake Mystic.

Stories were the second thing. An exciting rumor or prized piece of gossip crashed through town much like the river—with tremendous speed and often even greater force.

This was how, before anyone told her, Bailee knew the day she'd long waited for had finally arrived—the day of the game.

It was a day made of golden sunlight and leaves that crunched underfoot. Smoke rose like wayward spirits from newly awakened chimneys, and the chill that lingered on the breeze promised colder days to come. Jack-o'-lanterns sat plump and patient on porch steps, awaiting nightfall for their time to shine. Halloween had come, and while costumes and the night's potential candy haul preoccupied the minds of most kids at Beckett Elementary, the sixth graders thought only of the Bellwoods Game.

Bailee noticed the whispers first. Costumed heads bent together in deep discussion as she

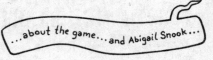

...about the game... and Abigail Snook...

Did you hear...?

It's happening tonight.

walked the halls. Notes were passed in a frenzy during second-period science. The lunchroom buzzed with phone notifications and an electric excitement that even managed to catch the attention of Mr. Owens, Beckett's oldest and most oblivious teacher. He was notorious for putting students to sleep with his spontaneous, long-winded stories. He was also wildly accident-prone. Being jolted out of a stupor by the sound of his scale-model solar system crashing to the ground was a nearly everyday occurrence. As were his gruesome paper cuts. No one could recall the last time Mr. Owens's hands weren't covered in bandages. The unexpected stories and bouts of chaos made his classes almost bearable, but only almost.

"Let's see what all the fuss is about." Mr. Owens motioned for Erica Livingstone to hand over her phone.

Bailee looked up from her book, a battered paperback with a ghost on the cover, as Erica eyed Mr. Owens's outstretched hand, her expression wary. Then, with a wince, she surrendered her phone. Mr. Owens fumbled it. Everyone braced themselves, waiting for the phone to smash to bits on the floor. But luck was on Owens's side today. And Erica's. He recovered his grip. Then he squinted at the screen. He looked as if he was about to say something, but just then a group of fifth graders began throwing pudding cups at one another. He gave the phone back to Erica and shuffled off toward the commotion. His threats of detention went unheard over the sounds of splatting pudding.

Bailee tapped her phone and brought up Erica's profile. Among the calls for social justice and group pics with friends was an odd post.

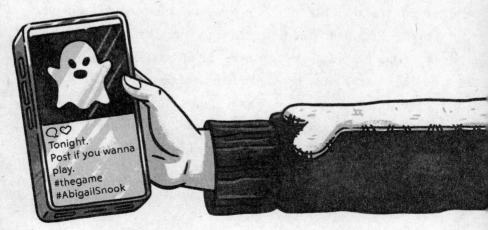

Stories flew fast and wild all afternoon with one thing in common—Abigail Snook. Everyone knew about her, even those who didn't know about the game. Her story was the town's most infamous tragedy. Many years ago, Abigail went into the woods behind Beckett Elementary and never came out. People said she'd been playing a game. One she'd never finished. Long after the sting of the girl's disappearance had faded, the students at Beckett Elementary still spoke of her. According to the legends, Abigail wasn't gone. Her spirit remained, doomed to roam the woods every Halloween night. She was unable to rest, kids said, until she finished her game. And, for that, she needed others to play.

Some refused to set foot in the woods after they heard the stories—unless on a dare, of course. Everyone knew coming face-to-face with a ghost would be preferable to the endless teasing they'd receive for wimping out on a dare. But despite the stories, the woods were safe—most of the time. Halloween night was the only time safety was not guaranteed, and everyone at Beckett Elementary knew to stay clear of the woods on that day. All but a select group—the ones who played the game.

More and more posts like Erica's appeared in Bailee's social feeds as the day wore on. Excitement grew too. By the time the last bell rang, Beckett felt like an overfilled balloon, ready to pop.

Bailee was excited too. She just didn't have anyone to share it with right now.

The final bell rang. Bailee knelt on the ground in front of her locker, piling books into her backpack. She pushed up the sleeves of her black sweater where felt patches shaped like bones had been stitched on to create skeleton arms. The sweater matched a pair of dusty-black jeans, also decorated with cotton bones.

She was struggling with a bulky math textbook when someone cleared their throat behind her.

"Hi, Madison," said Bailee. She didn't need to turn around to know who was hovering over her shoulder.

"So, you might have already heard, but everyone is meeting at Potts later. *For the game.*" Madison whispered this last part, words coming all in a rush.

Classic Madison. Right down to business.

Bailee wrestled the last of her books into her bag, grateful for an excuse to avoid Madison's gaze. "I saw the posts. I thought maybe the game had moved online or something. I . . . I wasn't sure I was invited." *Because no one wants me there.* Bailee kept that last part to herself.

"Of course you're invited! The whole class should be there, barring any interference. And the social posts are a decoy—my idea. Throw the adults off our trail," said Madison, adjusting her stylish glasses. She sparkled today in a dress of glittering blue. A tiara winked from the top of her head, and she held a homemade scepter in her hand, completing her Glinda the Good Witch look. *Wicked*, not *The Wizard of Oz*. Madison had been setting people straight about this all day.

Bailee smiled. Leave it to Madison to consider every angle. She always had a plan.

"I figure, if we pretend we're not playing the game at all, they'll be suspicious. But if they think the game's just a silly social media thing, they'll stop asking questions, right?"

"Worth a try."

"Exactly. Anything to keep parental types off our backs. Besides the posts, we're keeping things traditional this year. Less risk of getting caught like the fiasco two years ago."

Bailee opened her mouth to ask about the "fiasco," but Madison had already moved on. Such was the nature of the game. Just when you thought you'd heard every story, a new mystery jumped up and took you by surprise.

"So, consider this your invite, Bailee Heron. I'm this year's Keeper, so you know it's going to be fun."

Bailee's frown deepened. There was a lot of secrecy about the game, but she knew being picked as Keeper of the Game was a big deal—the next biggest deal to actually winning. How had Madison, Beckett's biggest chatterbox, managed to keep this news a secret? Or, Bailee wondered with a twinge, had there been just one person Madison had neglected to tell?

Bailee turned to face her friend. Madison had her hands together, pleading.

"It's just . . . after what happened—"

"This is different," Madison cut in. "This is *after school*. They can't keep us out of the woods then." Madison's voice was light, but Bailee noticed how her friend's eyes didn't quite meet her own.

An awkward silence pooled between them, one that had become familiar the past few weeks. Bailee used to think of herself and Madison as two neighboring pieces from the same puzzle; they fit together just right. But lately Bailee couldn't shake the feeling something unspoken had wedged between them.

"Seriously, please come," Madison said finally. "You need to start having some fun again."

"Me, no fun?" Bailee protested. "What do you call all this?" Bailee gestured to the textbooks and spooky novels spilling out of her bag.

Madison shuddered. "Homework and horror? Not my idea of fun, thanks."

Bailee poked out her tongue.

"Speaking of spine-chilling tales, wasn't that your story that Ms. Chivers read aloud in class today? I remember when you wrote it. We spent hours coming up with the perfect name for your Victorian ghost."

"The Wailing Widow," said Bailee.

"I preferred the Sad Lady Who Should Just Move On with

Her Afterlife," Madison teased. "Why did she say the author wanted to be anonymous?"

Bailee frowned. "The ending needs work."

She hadn't wanted Ms. Chivers to read her story to the class. It was an old one and not quite finished, in Bailee's opinion. She had ripped it out of an old notebook the morning the assignment was due because she hadn't been able to come up with anything new. Normally Bailee jumped at any excuse to write. She had a closet filled with notebooks, all crammed full of stories. They used to come to her effortlessly, not at all like when she tried to hit a baseball or make her clarinet do anything other than honk. But lately, it was like all the stories that once floated around her brain had drifted away.

"Well, you can always change the ending, if you want. But I thought your story was great!"

"You had your hands over your ears, like, the whole time," Bailee pointed out.

"That's only because it was so scary! You know I have a low spooky tolerance. Even so, I'd rather listen to a thousand of your stories before hearing another one of Oliver's weird poems about dill pickles. Chivers thinks they're funny, but I don't get them. . . ."

"Pickle poetry isn't for everyone." Bailee zipped up her backpack and shouldered it with a grunt. She trudged toward the school doors with Madison in tow.

Kids crowded the halls of Beckett Elementary. Voices

echoed. Shoes squeaked. Someone called Madison's name. She smiled and waved as they went by. Beside the front doors, a group of girls stood in a tight circle. Like Madison, they too were dressed as witches, but more traditional versions.

"Appropriate costumes for those three," Bailee muttered.

One of the girls, Gabby Millman, spotted their approach. She scowled in Bailee's direction. Then she put on a cold smile. She raised a hand to wave.

"Mads!" Gabby shouted. As if Bailee weren't even there.

Madison held up a hand, signaling for Gabby to wait. She turned to Bailee. "If you don't want to come tonight, I get it. But you've been looking forward to the game since forever. I'd hate for you to miss out because . . . you know." Madison fiddled with a silver ring on her little finger, eyes flicking toward Gabby.

Bailee stared at the floor. Madison was right. This was their year, their one shot at playing the game. But Madison had nothing to worry about. Bailee had no intention of missing out. If anything, Gabby's caustic stare only made her more determined to play.

And win.

"Come on, Mads," Bailee said in a light tone that wasn't at all like how she felt. "You know I wouldn't miss the game. Not for all the wicked witches in the world." She rolled her eyes in Gabby's direction.

Madison beamed. "Four thirty. We're meeting at Potts by the edge of the woods. Don't tell anyone, obviously. And don't forget, you have to bring—"

"Something to sacrifice if I want to play. I know," said Bailee.

Madison bounded away, joining Gabby, and the other two girls, Riley and Tate. Somebody must have cracked a joke because all four erupted into giggles as they stepped out the school's front door into bright October sunshine.

Once, Bailee would have joined them. But today she turned and slipped out a side door.

CHAPTER 2
TRADITIONS

Outside was quiet after the buzzing hallway. The sky overhead was an endless sort of blue, and the breeze smelled pleasantly of damp earth. Bailee breathed in the smell of autumn. But not even her favorite season could erase the image of Gabby's scowl. She shook her head, pushing the thought away. She imagined stuffing the thought in a box and tucking it in a dark corner of her mind, where she wouldn't have to deal with it anymore. If the box were real, she'd scrawl the words *Stuff I'd Rather Not Think About* on the side and tape it up tight.

Rounding a corner brought the front of the school into view. Students hurried to buses while others stood around in groups, laughing and soaking up the late October warmth.

Bailee ignored the crowd and hurried to the bike rack. She

fished around in her pocket for her lock key. Then she felt a small tap on her shoulder.

She jumped, almost tripping over her own feet. She whirled around and found herself looking at the smiling face of Noah Davies.

"Whoa, sorry!" he said. "I should know better than to sneak up on people. Especially when everyone has ghosts on the brain." He adjusted a pair of homemade lensless glasses. He wore a long white lab coat, artfully spattered with fake blood. A fancy pen was clipped to a pocket over his heart.

"Worse. In that getup, I thought you were Mr. Owens with a last-minute biology assignment," Bailee said. Noah was the new kid in town. Bailee didn't know much about him except that he got along with just about everyone but often spent lunchtime sitting alone. She never saw him without his pocket-sized notebook, always scribbling away. She had wondered if he liked writing stories, like her, but hadn't gotten around to asking. There had been bigger things on her mind.

Noah looked down, considering his costume. "I think Owens's lab coat is usually a *bit* bloodier than this one. The guy averages, like, five paper cuts per class. But I was wondering, do you have time to talk?"

"Depends. You looking for volunteers to experiment on?" Bailee eyed his costume again.

Noah leaned in close, eyes darting from left to right. "No. It's about . . . *the game*. It's happening tonight, right? Oh, and I'm Noah, by the way—"

"Noah, I know who you are. You've been sitting in front of me for the past two months. Your family just moved into that old place down on Fifth, right?"

"News sure gets around."

Does it ever. Out loud she said, "My nan's got this thing about old houses. She's always liked yours. You should hear the way she goes on about what a great job your parents are doing, fixing it up."

"My parents would love to hear that. They've been working on the place around the clock. Well, my dad mostly. Mom is busy setting up her new practice. The house was such a wreck, but it's not so bad now that the spiders have relocated to the attic. Most of them anyway." Noah shivered.

"It's because you're down by the river. Spiders can't resist waterfront property."

"Great. There goes my dream of living spider-free," said Noah. "When I was little, my cousin told me that spiders could grow to be as big as dogs. I knew he was lying. But they've given me the creeps ever since." He shivered again.

"Brutal. My cousins never gave me phobias, just hand-me-down clothes."

Noah laughed. He rummaged in his backpack while Bailee unlocked her bike. He produced a small notepad with a spiral coil running through the top, the same one he always carried. He flipped to a blank page, then plucked the pen out of his bloody lab-coat pocket. "I hear you're an expert on the Bellwoods Game."

"Wait, are you writing something about the game?" Bailee's eyes darted around, looking for watching eyes. All the kids in Fall Hollow knew about the game, of course, but that didn't make it any less of a secret. The last thing Bailee's reputation needed right now was to be seen spilling secrets.

"Not exactly." Noah adjusted his fake glasses. "I'm trying to persuade Ms. Chivers to start a school paper. For my first feature, I'm writing about Abigail Snook. I've read what's online and in the library's archive, but I still have so many questions. All anyone at school can tell me are ghost stories. They say kids have *seen* her during the game. I asked Madison, but no one on the Committee will say a word. She says it would *violate the rules of the game*." He imitated Madison's fast-paced way of speaking.

"Well, you're off to a good start. I didn't know Madison was on the Committee until a few minutes ago, and she's, like—" Bailee felt her cheeks burn. She had almost said that Madison was the only person who talked to her anymore. "My friend," she finished, flustered.

Noah shrugged. "My dad says I have a knack for finding stuff out. But my sister just says I'm nosy."

Bailee gave an amused snort. She pushed her bike toward home. Noah kept pace beside her.

"Why come to me?"

Noah grinned. "Madison couldn't tell me about the game, but she might have pointed me in the direction of someone who could."

"That sounds like Madison." Bailee's best friend was a stickler for rules, but if a loophole was to be found, Madison was sure to find one.

"Plus, I figure the girl with her nose jammed in a horror novel twenty-four seven must be an expert on Fall Hollow's resident ghost."

Bailee studied the boy next to her. He'd clearly been keeping an eye on his classmates.

She looked around again before continuing. "You didn't hear it from me, okay?"

Noah nodded, pen twitching.

"Okay. The game's an old Beckett Elementary tradition, going back years and years. Abigail Snook was supposedly playing it the night she disappeared. Problem is, she never actually finished. Legend says she returns every Halloween, on the anniversary of her disappearance. She's cursed to play an endless game—trying to win her freedom from the woods. To do that, she needs Beckett kids to play with her."

"So what exactly *is* the game?" Noah wrote furiously as they walked.

"It has to do with the old bell out in the woods. Three players are chosen to race to the bell. The one who rings it first banishes Abigail's spirit and keeps Fall Hollow safe for one more year."

"And what happens if someone *doesn't* ring the bell?"

"Then Abigail Snook will go free and unleash her wrath on the whole town," said Bailee with a grin. "No big deal."

"Spooky. What's a bell doing all the way out in the woods anyway?"

Bailee paused. She had never thought of the bell's existence as strange before. Much like the legends about Abigail Snook, it had always just been there. Then she had an idea. "I could ask my nan. She knows just about everything."

"Sounds like I need to meet your nan." Noah flipped through his notebook, showing Bailee page after page filled with questions. "Here's a good one," he said, tapping on a hasty scribble. "Why do only sixth graders play?"

"Well, Abigail was in the sixth grade when she disappeared—maybe that's why? It's just always been that way, kind of like . . ."

"A tradition?" Noah finished.

"Exactly."

The afternoon sun warmed the backs of their legs as they crossed the bridge at Main Street. They walked in silence, Bailee pushing her bike while Noah jotted down thoughts. Around them, other Beckett students laughed and blasted music from their phones. For a moment Bailee felt like part of it all, a regular kid walking home with a friend. It was a normal sort of feeling. A feeling she missed.

But she didn't want to think about that.

"Did you have any traditions at your old school?" Bailee asked.

Noah paused, looking thoughtful. "Some, I guess. Our class always played a prank on our teacher during the last week before summer vacation. Nothing mean, of course. We had a pretty good soccer team, too, and they always won regionals. It was a good school. For the most part." He suddenly sounded far away. He had a familiar look on his face, one much like Bailee had been wearing lately. Maybe Bailee wasn't the only one trying not to think of the way things used to be.

"But we didn't have anything like the Bellwoods Game." Noah's attention was back on Bailee. "Secret meetups and Committees? Presents for ghosts—"

"Gifts," she corrected.

"Right. What's the deal with the gifts?"

"They're sort of like . . . protection. Supposedly if a player gets caught by the ghost of Abigail Snook during the game, they can buy safe passage out of the woods with a gift."

Noah nodded, copying down every word. "Does it work? Do they keep kids safe?"

"Depends on which stories you want to believe. I don't think anyone has gone missing since Abigail Snook, so . . . maybe? But I did hear one about a kid who played the game without one. A long time ago."

"What happened?" Noah asked, eyes bright with curiosity.

Bailee grinned. She knew the story well. She'd written it

down in a special journal, one reserved solely for Bellwoods stories. It was one of Bailee's most prized possessions, a collection of every spine-tingling legend and frightful rumor about the Bellwoods Game that had ever circulated through Beckett Elementary.

Bailee didn't have her journal with her now, but she knew the story well enough. She took a deep breath and put on the serious face she reserved for telling tales. Then she began. "He was a loud kid, the kind always getting in trouble for talking. He didn't believe in Abigail's ghost. Said the stories were baloney and he was going to play the game and prove it. So, on Halloween night, after he was chosen to play, he went into the woods without a gift. He was gone for a long time. The other two players came back, but there was no sign of the boy. There were sounds, though. Awful, terrifying sounds."

"Creepy," said Noah, taking notes as Bailee spoke.

"It was dark when he returned, stumbling out of the woods in a daze. There was nothing wrong with him otherwise. There wasn't even any mud on his shoes or scratches on his arms or face, which was weird considering this kid had been running around the woods in the dark. But all that mattered was he'd come out of the woods in one piece. At least that's what people thought at first. In the days following, the boy acted strange—quiet. Kids tried to get him to talk about what happened in the woods. But he couldn't. Not anymore."

"Why not?"

Bailee let her bike come to rest beside her. "Because if you don't have a gift to sacrifice during the game, Abigail will find something to *take* instead."

Noah swallowed hard. "What did she take?" He wasn't writing anymore. He was looking at Bailee, eyes wide.

She let the moment linger.

"His tongue," she finished finally, dropping the ending like a ton of bricks. Her mouth twitched into a grin.

Noah looked at her, stunned. Then he laughed. "Gross."

"Totally." Bailee pushed her bike. "But I doubt that really happened."

"But people believe this stuff, right? After hearing the stories, the game seems . . ."

"Scary? Dangerous?"

"Both! I mean, if any of this is true, why play?"

It was a good question. Bailee didn't believe the stories about the woods, not really. But it was fun to imagine they could be true. Stories had the power to transform the ordinary into something . . . more. They could turn a boring forest into a place where ghosts roamed or a kids' game into a powerful tradition that protected the town from harm. As far as Bailee was concerned, stories were a sort of magic. Playing the Bellwoods Game felt like a chance to be part of one of her favorite spooky tales. That's why she wanted to play. One reason, anyway. But she wasn't about to tell Noah all that.

"Maybe it's the mystery," she said finally. "If you want to

know what's true and what isn't, playing the game is the only way to know for sure. You can't ask the older kids. Most of the time they pretend they don't even know what you're talking about. Or tell you a story so wild, it couldn't possibly be true. If you want to know for sure, you have to find out for yourself. Besides," she added, "whoever wins the game is granted legendary status at Beckett."

"You're kidding."

"Hey, some schools are all about sports. Here at Beckett, the coolest kids survive a night in the woods with a ghost."

Noah laughed. "So you're going to play, then?"

"I—ow!" Bailee cried.

Someone had knocked into her from behind. The boy responsible kept walking as if he hadn't noticed.

"Hey!" shouted Noah. But the other boy pretended not to hear.

Bailee said nothing. She glared after her classmate, Luca Shaw. She watched him fall into step beside another boy, Fenwick Leer. Luca whispered to Fen. Their heads swiveled toward Bailee. Fen frowned and turned away.

Bailee felt her cheeks burn. So much for feeling normal.

"Are those two always so unpleasant?" Noah glared after the other boys.

Bailee's jaw clenched. Luca had always been a pest, the sort of kid who pointed and laughed when someone tripped over an untied shoelace. But Fen was different. He could be a troublemaker, sure, but he had never been mean. Not until recently.

She kicked a leg over her bike. "I need to get home."

Noah dropped the subject. "Yeah, of course. So . . . I'll see you at Potts later?"

Bailee paused, staring at the backs of Fen and Luca. If they thought hassling her would keep her away from the game tonight, they were wrong. Dead wrong.

"Definitely."

Noah grinned, then hurried off to catch up with their classmates Beth Yang and Desmond Cody, no doubt after more information about Abigail Snook.

Bailee stood up on her pedals. She pumped her legs up and down, blazing past Fen and Luca.

She thought she heard someone call her name. She didn't look back.

CHAPTER 3
DARES AND SUPERSTITIONS

Bailee's legs ached as she blazed down Maple Street. She sped past the library, its wide concrete steps piled high with pumpkins and hay bales. Bailee's favorite ice cream shop, The Freeze, sat next door. In the summer, the line for soft-serve usually stretched all the way down the street. Today it sat dark and empty. A little sign hung on the glass door reading CLOSED FOR THE SEASON. Bailee turned onto Larkspur Road, one of her favorite streets, lined with old houses. Her breath caught ragged in her chest, but she pushed for more speed. On the pavement below, her shadow glided along beside her.

"Why can't they let it go?" she murmured to her shadow-self. But, if her shadow had any answers, it didn't say.

Things should have blown over by now. Bailee and Fen

had been friends since kindergarten, and in all the time she'd known him, he wasn't one to hold a grudge. They'd fought before, but after a few hours he'd always been back to his normal joke-cracking self. But for some reason, things didn't go back to normal this time. They got worse.

If only he'd never agreed to that dare.

It all started three weeks ago with a picture of a fallen tree, stretched out across the top of Silver Falls like a precarious bridge. Herschel Ford had taken it while out hiking with his family. It got sent around to almost everyone in class accompanied by a challenge: dare you to walk across.

Most kids laughed off the obviously dangerous dare. But not Fen. He was no stranger to getting into trouble and had a particular weakness for dares. Recently, the trouble he found himself in had grown more frequent and the dares he accepted far more reckless. Fen announced he would walk across the fallen tree during their next recess. Anyone who didn't believe he could do it was invited to watch and see for themselves.

Bailee had planned to be among the excited onlookers that day. She'd started thinking of it as the *Day of the Dare*. But she didn't make it to the falls. Principal Bright had found her first.

Fen never completed his dare. By the time he and his eager audience arrived at the falls, Bright was there waiting for them. Nearly the whole sixth grade ended up with detention that day. Fen, who'd already burned through Bright's allowance of goodwill for the year, had been given a three-day suspension for even thinking about attempting something so dangerous. There was a rumor floating around that if Fen screwed up one more time, he'd be kicked out of Beckett for good.

How had Bright known about the dare? Someone had told, that much was clear. No one knew for sure, but Bailee became the number one suspect. Several students reported seeing her talking to Principal Bright right before the foiled dare. Then she disappeared for the rest of the afternoon with no explanation. Who else could have ratted, if not Bailee? None of her classmates bothered to ask what she and Bright had *really* spoken about on the Day of the Dare. They weren't interested. Least of all Fen. He hadn't said a word to Bailee since returning from his suspension, despite her best efforts to defend herself. As far as he was concerned, their friendship was over.

Fen's anger proved contagious. One by one, her classmates came down with Bailee-itis. People avoided her in the halls and at recess. Her friendly greetings were ignored. Her tentative questions hung in the air, unanswered. It was like she'd become invisible. But her classmates could see her—Bailee knew this for sure. Why else did whispered conversations suddenly stop whenever she walked by?

Bailee took a deep breath and let it out slowly as she rounded onto Oak Lane.

At least Madison was still speaking to her. But Bailee saw her best friend less and less these days. Madison was often busy with after-school activities or hanging out with other friends from the grade above them. Maybe Bailee was just imagining things, but she felt a distance growing between them. Was this a normal part of getting older? Or, she wondered with a twinge, maybe even Madison wasn't immune to all the Bailee-hate going around.

Bailee sailed down a small slope. Then she sucked in a big gulp of air. She let her bike slow to a smooth coast as Potts Cemetery sprang into view.

It was an old kind of cemetery. It sat on a hill, framed by the Bellwoods with long grass growing in tangles and a smattering of grayish white gravestones. Some of the stones slouched to the side as if tired from years of standing upright. Most had been there so long, the names had worn clear away.

While some of her classmates (especially Madison) thought the place was creepy, Bailee found Potts peaceful. The scari-

est thing she'd ever come across was a harmless garter snake who'd startled her after it slithered out from behind a gravestone while she and Fen were exploring. That had been years ago now. Back then, she and Fen used to pretend they were ghost hunters, searching the cemetery for proof of the afterlife. Or they biked past as fast as they could, pretending to outrun a pack of hungry zombies who'd risen from the cemetery in

search of fresh brains. Bailee pedaled extra hard now, imagining a zombie horde lurching after her, just like she and Fen had once done.

Bailee winced and shoved the memory away. Another one for her imaginary box of stuff she'd rather not think about.

Her bike rolled into the shade of the tall oaks that edged the cemetery. She let her breath out with a *whoosh*. It was a silly superstition. But it was bad luck if you forgot to hold your breath while passing a graveyard. Everyone knew that. The last thing Bailee needed these days was more bad luck. Not on the day of the game.

Like Potts, Bailee's house was perched on a small hill, nestled against the Bellwoods. As Bailee rolled up, she spied her grandmother in the driveway, standing next to a wheelbarrow with a small hatchet in hand. Pieces of firewood lay scattered around. Nan caught sight of Bailee and gave a wave. Then she bent to pick up a small piece of wood and placed it on a wide, wellworn log. Then there was a loud *THWACK* as Nan brought the hatchet down on it, splitting off a thin piece.

Bailee swung her leg over her bike and walked it up the driveway. Her tires crunched on the gravel as she brought her bike to rest against the side of the house.

THWACK!

"Nan!" called Bailee, out of breath. She hurried toward her grandmother. "I don't think chopping wood is on Mom's list of approved activities!"

"Oh, hush," said Nan, hacking off another small chunk from the log. "If it was up to your mom, I'd never leave the house. But Benny Marsh just dropped off a load of firewood, and we need to split some for kindling. Makes sense to do that now before putting it all away." She brushed a sleeve across her brow. "Besides, I'm feeling fine."

Bailee tugged on the frayed cuff of her sweater. Nan was the toughest grandmother she knew, but that didn't keep Bailee from worrying about her, especially these days. "You're supposed to be taking it easy," she said.

"Good thing you're here to help, then," said Nan, eyes

crinkling in the corners as she smiled. "Hope you're not too tired from all that learning today."

"I'm exhausted, now that you mention it." Bailee gave an exaggerated groan. "Would you believe, I had to outrun a pack of zombies out by Potts on my way home?"

"Must have spotted all those books poking out of your backpack and figured you had brains to spare." Nan winked.

"That must have been it." Bailee grinned. She and Nan were always doing this, dressing up their day in a little make-believe.

Bailee knelt to gather the pieces of split wood littering the ground. She piled them into the wheelbarrow, then scooped up more in her arms, careful to avoid the splintered bits. She trudged around the back of the house toward the woodshed. Nan followed, pushing the loaded-up wheelbarrow.

The backyard was shaded by the Bellwoods. Leaves littered the grass while more fell from the trees. Bailee had grown up next to the woods, and despite all the stories, she'd never felt afraid. Still, watching the woods now, she couldn't help but feel that a change had come over it, something she couldn't describe.

She dropped her bundle of firewood on the neatly stacked pile in the shed. Suddenly, a dark shape shot out from a nearby tangle of bushes and darted past her feet. Bailee stumbled back in surprise. She watched as it bolted across the grass and settled in the shadows of Bailee's back deck. A pair of yellow eyes, round and bright like moons, stared at her.

"Magic!" she said, hand to her heart. "You almost made me jump out of my skin."

"By the look of you, I'd say he succeeded," said Nan, eyeing Bailee's skeleton costume. Bailee laughed.

Magic was Nan's cat. He'd shown up on her doorstep years ago, all skin and bones and missing a chunk from one ear. Now he spent most of his time curled up beside Nan's woodstove and enjoying regularly scheduled meals. But he still liked to come and go as he pleased. Nan said there was a little wild left in him.

"You silly creature," said Nan as the skinny black cat scurried over to her and rubbed against her shin. "I've been looking everywhere for you. After all these years, you still haven't figured out that you're supposed to be an indoor cat."

"He can't resist the woods."

"Guess not. He must have snuck out when

your mom left for work this morning." Nan parked the wheel-barrow next to the woodshed. She massaged her left arm, flexing the fingers. She'd been doing that a lot lately.

"When's Mom home?" Bailee asked.

Nan frowned. "Not until late tonight. They asked her to stay a few extra hours. Halloween's a busy time."

"She's always staying late," said Bailee, making a face.

"Her loss. She's missing out on the firewood-stacking fun. Guess I'll have to pass hatchet duty over to you."

"That's an accident waiting to happen," Bailee scoffed.

Nan smiled. "Too true. With your luck, we'll end up having to visit your mom at the hospital. The upside is, you'll probably fit in better with your new zombie friends if you've got a few stitches." The corners of Nan's eyes crinkled again.

Bailee wanted to laugh. She loved joking around with Nan. They could go on for hours, making up stories and riffing off each other. But today, mention of the hospital made Bailee's stomach turn. Memories flooded her mind, taking her back to her last visit—the Day of the Dare.

Bailee had been just about to slip into the woods, on her way to the falls. She was sure Fen would chicken out on his dare, and she wanted to be there to tease him. But before she could step foot off school grounds, Principal Bright appeared at her elbow. He wasn't there to reprimand her about sneaking into the woods. He'd come to deliver difficult news; Nan was in the hospital.

It'd been a terrifying afternoon, the worst of Bailee's life. Nan had what the doctor called a transient ischemic attack, or a TIA. It was like a stroke, but the symptoms passed very quickly. The doctor explained that, for a little while following the attack, Nan might feel extra tired or confused. He said there was a chance her muscles might not work quite as well or could tingle with a "pins and needles" feeling, the sort Bailee got when she sat with her foot tucked under her too long. But, the doctor assured them, after some rest, Nan would be back to her usual self. Bailee knew her nan was in good hands, her mom being a nurse and all. But the doctor also said that people who had TIAs were at risk of having a more serious stroke later. If that happened, Bailee worried Nan might not be okay afterward. Her worries hung over her like a heavy cloud, one she couldn't shake.

"Say, what's Madison up to these days?" said Nan, noting the glum look on Bailee's face. "She hasn't been by in a while. She knows I depend on her for my daily dose of Fall Hollow news. You two still going trick-or-treating together tonight?"

"Uh . . . yeah." Bailee knelt to restack part of the woodpile, hoping Nan didn't catch the wave of guilt that crossed her face.

It was one thing to joke around about zombies. But pretending she and Madison were going trick-or-treating when they had other plans wasn't a silly story; it was a lie.

"Good. One of us should have a little fun tonight." Nan got up from the porch step and stretched. Then she winced and put a hand to her back.

"Nan! Are you okay?" Bailee rushed toward her grand-mother.

Nan waved her away. "No need to worry. I just overdid it working at the old house earlier."

Bailee's gaze traveled across the street to where a roof poked through the red and yellow trees.

Bailee had lived across the street from her grandmother since she was a baby. But she wouldn't for much longer. After the TIA, Nan had decided the old house was too much for her. Bailee's parents agreed. So Nan moved into the bedroom down the hall from Bailee. But Nan's old house was still filled with furniture, knickknacks, and things from when Bailee's mom and aunt were little girls. Over the past couple weeks, they'd spent every spare moment sorting through the old house, deciding what would be kept and what would be donated. Once Nan's house was empty, it would be sold.

"You should have waited. I could have helped," said Bailee.

"Don't worry, there's lots more packing to do. I haven't even touched your aunt's room yet. I asked if she wanted to keep any of her old things. But she's not interested."

"I don't even remember the last time she visited."

"It's been a long time. She couldn't wait to leave home when she was old enough. She's still convinced the town is haunted. Of all the silly things . . ." Nan gave an exasperated shake of her head.

Bailee had heard this about her aunt before. Fall Hollow

was home to plenty of spooky stories; that was no secret. But to leave home because of them and refuse to return? That was a whole other level of fear, one Bailee couldn't understand.

"So her belongings are going to donation," said Nan, reaching down to give Magic a pat. "Stuff's been sitting, collecting dust for years. Might as well go to someone who can use it."

"Makes sense."

Magic pawed at Nan and gave a plaintive meow.

"But there's plenty of time for all that later. Right now, we've got to get this guy fed. You too." Nan pointed at Bailee. "You're wasting away. Look at you, you're just bones!" said Nan, plucking at Bailee's skeleton costume.

Bailee grinned and followed Nan and Magic into the house.

CHAPTER 4
NAN'S TALE

"You have a cobweb in your hair," said Nan.

"Ah, get it!" said Bailee. She froze, a spoonful of soup halfway to her mouth. Nan plucked a tangled gray wisp from her hair, then walked over to the kitchen door leading to the back deck. She deposited the wisp outside. Beside the door, Magic gulped his dinner down, purring between mouthfuls.

"Guess we didn't need to do any Halloween decorating this year. The spiders have it covered," Nan said.

"They must celebrate all year long," said Bailee.

Bailee had changed into a regular pair of jeans and a warm pullover sweater. Her bone costume sat conspicuously by the front door, folded next to her backpack. She had also stashed her Bellwoods journal inside. She'd need it later for the game.

Bailee had told Nan she needed to head out right after dinner to meet up with Madison. What they were meeting up for, Bailee had been careful not to specify.

"Your dad called earlier." Nan peered at Bailee over the top of her mug of steaming tea.

Bailee frowned. "He couldn't have waited until after I got home from school?"

"He says he's been trying. Cell reception is bad up there. Even texts won't go through most of the time."

"Is he still coming home next week?" Bailee was careful to keep her voice flat. She knew better than to get her hopes up at this point.

Nan sighed. "His contract's been extended another couple of weeks. It's good news, really. Sounds like they're happy with him. He says they might even have a full-time position available, one that will let him work from home. But of course we'll have to wait and see."

Bailee's mouth pressed into a straight line.

"He said he misses all of us and wanted me to wish you a happy Halloween. You're supposed to send him a picture of you in your costume," said Nan, trying her best to soften the disappointing message.

Bailee didn't say anything, just stirred her soup as if it were the most fascinating activity in the world.

Her dad was an accountant. He'd once worked for a factory that made machine parts just outside of town. But two years ago, it closed, leaving many in Fall Hollow without jobs.

Since then, Bailee's dad had worked for different places on short contracts. His most recent position took him to a remote town five hours away, helping with a large audit. Bailee knew his contract getting extended was a good sign, especially if a more permanent position was on the horizon. It meant Bailee's mom might be able to cut back on extra shifts at the hospital. It meant a likely end to her parents' worried whispering behind closed doors late at night. But it also meant, for now, Bailee and Nan ate most dinners alone.

"Why don't you tell me about your day?" said Nan, changing the subject.

Bailee frowned. School was another touchy topic these days. But she had to admit, today hadn't been all bad. She thought back to her walk home with Noah and his questions about the game.

"Actually, I have a question for you. You know pretty much everything, right?"

"I wouldn't say that. In fact, the older I get, the less I seem to know." Nan's eyes crinkled in the corners.

"I mean about local stuff. Fall Hollow stuff," said Bailee. She spooned the last of her soup into her mouth and pushed the bowl aside.

"Such as?" Nan raised an eyebrow.

"Like, about the bell. The one in the woods." Bailee tried to sound casual. "A boy from class was asking about it. He's new here. His family moved into that house you like, the one down on Fifth."

"The old yellow brick place, that's right," Nan said. "I drove by the other day and saw they had new windows put in and the trim all painted fresh. So nice to see that home loved again. And I'm glad you're making new friends."

Bailee shrugged. "He had some questions about the bell. I told him that if anyone knew, you would."

Nan watched the Bellwoods swaying in the breeze through the kitchen window. Magic finished eating and jumped onto Nan's lap. She scratched behind his ears, then took a deep breath, the way she always did when a story was brewing.

Bailee settled in.

"The bell is one of Fall Hollow's biggest mysteries," Nan began. "It's been out in the woods for as long as anyone can remember. But no one really knows who put it there." Nan fell silent, sipping her tea.

"But . . . ," Bailee prompted.

"But," Nan continued, "*why* the bell was put there is a different story."

"That's more like it," said Bailee.

Nan went on. "Bells are powerful objects. They're often used to communicate. The sound of a ringing bell may call us forth. Or alert us to danger. Some even believe ringing a bell can rid spaces of harmful spirits."

"Really?" asked Bailee.

Nan shrugged. "That's what some people think. According to old legends, there's one place in Fall Hollow where a bell might be particularly useful."

"The Bellwoods?" Bailee guessed, right on cue.

"Exactly." Nan's eyes crinkled at the corners again. "People in Fall Hollow have always been a superstitious bunch, and stories about spirits haunting the Bellwoods are as old as the town itself. Long ago, people passing through the woods rang the bell in order to protect themselves."

"Did it work? Does the bell keep spirits away?" Bailee asked.

Nan thought for a moment. "I think when it comes to superstitions, it's not whether they work or not; it's how much people *believe* they work. There are lots of traditions thought to protect against bad luck or supernatural forces. There's knocking on wood, throwing a pinch of salt over their shoulder—"

"Holding your breath when passing the cemetery, not walking under ladders or opening an umbrella in the house," Bailee added.

"Some even think this guy crossing their path is bad luck." Nan scratched Magic under the chin. "The bell isn't even the only superstition connected to the Bellwoods. According to old legends, travelers would also bring little trinkets into the woods, something to sacrifice in exchange for safe passage home, in case they happened upon any spirits."

Bailee couldn't help but think this sounded an awful lot like the supposedly secret game she and her friends were about to play. She made a mental note to relay all this to Noah later.

Nan continued. "I doubt many believe in the Bellwoods spirits anymore. The old legends are just a way to pass the time and convince tourists to stop and stay awhile. People aren't quite so fearful of the woods these days. At least, they weren't, until what happened to that poor Snook girl." Nan shook her head.

"Abigail Snook?" Bailee asked, hoping her voice sounded innocently curious and not at all like she was pumping Nan for information.

"Such a tragedy. Police knocked on our door the day after Abigail went missing, looking for any information we could give. But there was no sign of the girl—nothing credible, at any rate. What a terrible time that was for the town."

"Why? What happened?"

Nan sighed. "Fall Hollow has had its share of troubles, but the year following Abigail's disappearance was one bad thing after another. Crops shriveled and died in the fields. Businesses closed left and right. Neighbors who'd once gotten along started fighting. Family members stopped speaking. . . . Some said the town was cursed. Others blamed the Snook girl—can you believe it? A few even claimed to have seen her ghost roaming the woods. There were lots of stories like that."

"Really?" said Bailee, as if she hadn't heard that part before.

"Mm-hmm. Now, you know I love a good story, but some were hard on the Snook family. They were practically run out of town by rumors following Abigail's disappearance. Hardly a Snook left in the whole county now. Can't say I blame them."

Bailee frowned again. For as long as she could remember, Abigail had been a legend, just a ghost story kids told at sleepovers and around campfires for a thrill. But now, thinking of the people Abigail had left behind and how they must have felt—and continued to feel—about her disappearance, a knot of guilt formed in Bailee's stomach. What happened to Abigail wasn't just a story to them.

Bailee thought about her journal full of Bellwoods stories, tucked away in her backpack, ready for the game. "Do you think any of those stories were true, about Abigail?" she asked quietly.

Nan didn't speak for a moment, just watched the Bellwoods through the kitchen window. "I think stories have a way of revealing truths even if they're not true stories. Maybe people really did see strange sights in the Bellwoods. Or maybe the tales were just a way to express the fear and anxiety of the time, a way to make sense of all the unfortunate stuff that was happening—I can't say. There's a little truth hidden away in every story, I think. But what that is, well, that's a question we all have to ask ourselves." Nan yawned and stretched, signaling the end of her tale. Magic squeezed one eye open and reluctantly jumped down from her lap.

Bailee was quiet, letting Nan's words settle around her. The last part in particular echoed loudly in her mind.

Then her phone buzzed.

It was Madison. Time to leave.

"Thanks for the story, Nan. I'll pass it along to Noah." Bailee hugged her grandmother tight, then grabbed her empty bowl and deposited it in the kitchen sink. She made her way to the front door. She kneeled, slipping her journal out of her backpack and flipping to a blank page.

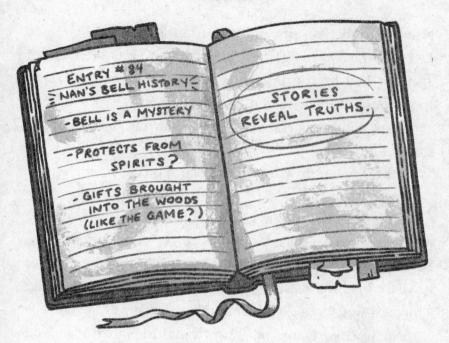

"You have your cell phone?" Nan asked, appearing in the doorway behind Bailee.

"Mm-hmm," Bailee said, slipping her journal back into her bag.

"And you won't be home too late?"

Bailee shook her head. This wasn't a lie. At least, she didn't think it would be. How long could the game last anyway? An hour? Two at the most? Maybe she'd even have time for some actual trick-or-treating after they were done. The idea made her feel lighter, like she wasn't really lying to Nan about her plans. Just leaving out some details.

Bailee wrapped her arms around her grandmother again.

Nan hugged back, warm and reassuring. Bailee hugged tighter. Just a couple weeks ago, she thought she'd never see her nan again. It had been a terrifying thought, more so than any spooky story. Part of her didn't want to let go.

But tonight was her one chance to play the game. And she couldn't be late.

Bailee reluctantly let go. She shrugged on her backpack and stepped out the door.

"Not so fast, mister." Nan snatched Magic up as he attempted to dash outside. "Halloween is too busy for cats to be out roaming. Too many cars. There might even be zombies or wicked Bellwoods spirits out there." Nan winked at Bailee. "You best watch out for all those things too, my dear."

"No worries, Nan. I'm always careful about traffic. And those last two are just stories. They don't scare me." Bailee gave her grandmother one last grin, then bounded down the front steps. She hopped on her bike and kicked off. Her wheels crunched along the gravel drive and switched to a smooth whir when they found the road.

CHAPTER 5
WHISPERS IN THE GRAVEYARD

Bailee was out of breath by the time she reached the cemetery. The sun hung low in the sky, and the earlier warmth was fading fast. Long purple shadows slanted from the pockmarked gravestones, and the leaves of the Bellwoods whispered in the brisk breeze.

Bailee dropped her bike on the cemetery's overgrown grass, front wheel spinning. She expected the cemetery to be crawling with her classmates, but the scruffy hill was silent and still. She hurried toward the tall wrought iron gate separating Fall Hollow's living from the long-deceased. It was secured by a heavy padlock and chain. Around the base of the gate, long, yellow grass, dry like straw, stuck up in tufts and swayed gently in the wind. Nothing else moved.

Had she misunderstood about where the game was taking place? She couldn't have the time wrong; Madison had been sending her updates all day. Bailee peered through the bars, straining for sounds of life. "Hello?" she called. Then she stumbled back in surprise.

A shape emerged from behind one of the gravestones.

"Ditch the bike in the bushes," a voice said. "And hurry. Game's about to start."

Bailee squinted. What she had mistaken for a living shadow was one of her classmates, Milo Mihalik. He gestured toward the woods, then retreated behind the gravestone, out of sight.

Bailee ran to her bike and wheeled it toward the woods. Thick bushes crowded the edge of the cemetery grounds, and as she drew near, she spied half a dozen other bikes hidden within. With some effort, she pushed hers under a shrub. Bailee slipped her backpack from her shoulders. She pulled out her journal and stuffed the slender notebook into the waistband of her jeans. Then she pushed her backpack into the bushes beside her bike for safekeeping.

She jogged back toward the gate, took hold of the bars, and pushed as hard as she could. It gave a rusty squeak, then gave way, creating a gap big enough for Bailee to slip through.

She hurried up the cemetery hill, careful to avoid tripping over the smaller grave markers hidden in the long grass. The sound of murmuring voices grew louder. As she crested the hill, her classmates came into view, crowded together in the shade of the Bellwoods. Kids laughed and chatted, standing in small groups among the gravestones. Bailee spotted Madison standing apart from the crowd, talking animatedly with two older kids. One, Jade Romero, carried a satchel over one shoulder and was nodding along as Madison spoke. The other, Arlo Jackson, wore a baseball cap pulled down low, arms crossed in front, regarding the scene with a grim look.

"Hey! Bailee!" came a voice.

Noah waved at her from the edge of the woods. He stood with Beth Yang and Eli Bannerman, pen and notepad in hand. Bailee waved back and drifted toward him, passing groups of her classmates as she went.

"My older brother said that a girl in his year was so messed up from playing the game, she stayed home from school for three weeks," whispered Emmy Sinclair as Bailee walked past.

"People really shouldn't play if they're that sensitive," sniffed Addison Van Beek in reply.

"I'm betting one of the players will totally lose it in there. Seeing them run out of the woods screaming will be the biggest laugh of the year," said Luca Shaw. He was standing with Fen and another boy, Brendan Boyd. They all chuckled, eyeing their fellow classmates, no doubt wondering which one of them would lose their cool if things got too spooky.

Bailee scowled as she strode past. Leave it to Fen and his friends to come to the game just to make fun of people.

"I heard that a few years ago one of the players was attacked by a whole flock of bats!" said Oliver Moore, waving his arms around for dramatic effect.

"A colony. A group of bats is called a colony," corrected Carmen Alverez, standing at Oliver's elbow. She wore heavy-duty hiking boots and clutched an extra-large flashlight in one hand.

"Right, right," said Oliver, brushing her comment away. "You know what that means?"

"Vampires?" guessed Alvin McNally.

"No. That would be *ridiculous*," said Oliver very seriously. "It means there are KILLER BATS in the woods!"

"And that's not ridiculous at all," Carmen said under her breath.

"That's nothing. My sister told me that, on the night of the game, the woods change," Min Zhou whispered. "The trees walk and rearrange themselves, totally under Abigail's command."

Oliver opened his mouth to reply, then caught sight of Bailee lingering nearby. More heads turned. The whole group fell silent.

Bailee kept walking. Then a new voice caught her attention.

"Who invited her?" the voice said.

"Who do you think?" whispered another.

Bailee turned. Gabby, Riley, and Tate were staring at her, eyes narrowed.

"I keep telling Mads to drop her, but she doesn't listen," grumbled Gabby.

"Do you think she tattled about the game?" Riley said.

"Wouldn't put it past her," replied Gabby. "She's such a two-face. *She ruins everything.*"

Bailee felt her face flush, and her fingers curled into fists. She wanted to march over and shout at them about how wrong they were. She'd almost done it once before, during recess. She'd overheard Gabby on the playground telling a group of their classmates that she saw Bailee talking to Principal Bright on the Day of the Dare. Bailee had to be the rat, Gabby had said. Bailee had stomped over, ready to set everyone straight. But the words she'd needed hadn't come. She'd ended up just standing there in front of them all, tongue-tied, looking more guilty than she had before.

So, today, she said nothing.

Bailee hurried past the girls, pretending not to have overheard. Luckily, Noah was all smiles as she drew near. At least someone was happy to see her.

"I was beginning to think you weren't coming," Noah called as Bailee approached. He stood next to an old gravestone. A faint inscription was barely legible between the moss and lichen.

"Old Greg here filling you in on all the ghostly gossip?" said Bailee, patting the gravestone like an old friend.

"I wish. That would be an interview to *die* for," Noah joked.

Bailee laughed, but her smile slipped as she noticed Beth and Eli hurry away. She tugged at her sweater sleeve. *Whatever*, she told herself. If she scared everyone off before the game even started, she'd have better odds of getting picked to play.

"What did I miss?" she asked Noah, pretending she didn't care about Beth and Eli's apparent allergy to her presence.

"Well, I've collected lots of stories about the game, the woods, and all the weird stuff that supposedly goes on in there," said Noah. He flipped through his notepad. "But not much information about Abigail. The real one, I mean. I've heard plenty about the ghost version."

"Who knows, maybe she'll appear tonight and you can interview her yourself."

Noah opened his mouth to reply but was interrupted.

"Five minutes, everyone! Then it's time to start," called Madison in her best impersonation of a teacher. She caught sight of Bailee and gave an excited wave before rejoining her conversation with Jade and Arlo.

"Who's Madison with? They look familiar," said Noah. He flipped to a new page in his notebook.

"You've probably seen them around school. That's Jade Romero," said Bailee, nodding at the girl. "And the other is Arlo Jackson. They're both in the grade above us."

Noah flipped through his notepad. "They must be the other members of the Committee, then. There are always three, right? The current year's Keeper of the Game, last year's Keeper, and last year's winner."

"Sounds right. I'm betting Jade's the former Keeper. She and Madison got close when they were in the spring musical last year. I'm sure she picked Mads to follow in her footsteps."

"So that leaves Arlo as last year's winner, then."

"Correct. Funny," said Bailee thoughtfully. "They don't look quite as excited about the game as everyone else." Arlo stood apart from the others, face grim. They kept shooting nervous looks at the woods. "I wonder what's up. Last I heard, everything was going great for Arlo. Their mom just won the lottery."

"You always hear about people winning the lottery, but I've never known anyone in real life who has," said Noah.

"It was a big deal. Happened at the perfect time too. The bookstore Arlo's mom owns was about to go out of business. Mrs. Jackson was worried they'd have to sell their house and move in with Arlo's grandpa over in Thornton. But now they won't have to. That's what Nan told me, anyway."

"Wow, people really know everything about everyone around here, huh?"

Bailee grinned. "Better get used to it."

"Sounds like Arlo's family lucked out."

"Maybe," said Bailee. "But they might have had more than luck on their side this past year."

Curiosity sparked in Noah's eyes, but before he could ask any more questions, Madison was back. She waved her arms at the crowd, and a hush fell over the cemetery.

"Welcome, everyone," she began. "It's time to play the Bellwoods Game!"

CHAPTER 6
THE BELLWOODS GAME

"Let's see some GHOSTS!" came a voice from the back of the crowd, sparking a burst of laughter.

Madison's eyes narrowed, and her mouth twitched into a frown. She had exchanged her sparkling good-witch costume for jeans, a warm jacket, and a scarf. She shot a warning look at the rowdy crowd before clearing her throat to continue.

"For anyone who doesn't already know, here with me is Jade Romero, last year's Keeper of the Game." Madison gestured to the tall girl with the satchel hanging from one shoulder.

Jade stepped forward and waved. "The Bellwoods Game is an annual tradition for Beckett Elementary students. According to legend, a student must play—and win—the Bellwoods

Game in order to keep Fall Hollow safe from the wrath of Abigail Snook. This year, playing falls to you all."

"Woo-hoo!" came another shout from the crowd. There were more giggles. The noise level in the cemetery began to rise.

"HEY!" yelled Arlo. The shout sliced through the chatter like a knife. "It might be called a game, but this is no joke. Everyone planning to volunteer to play needs to pay attention."

The laughter and chatter died.

Noah shot Bailee a questioning look. She shrugged. It wasn't like Arlo to yell. As far as she knew, Arlo never got worked up about anything. But today tense agitation radiated from them. In place of their usual easygoing smile was a grimace of worry. Arlo started to say something else but doubled over into a coughing fit instead. A minute passed and they went quiet again.

"As I was saying . . . ," said Jade after a beat, giving Arlo a look of concern. "One of the Keeper's most important tasks is looking after this." She held up a book in her hands. It was old and water-stained. The cover was torn and patched in several places, and peeling layers of yellowed tape coated the spine. A long cloth bookmark poked out from between the pages.

"Inside is a list of rules as well as the names of every player who has come before, going back years and years. It's the duty of the Keeper to guard and uphold the rules of the game and pass them on to those who will play after us. It's my pleasure to pass the book along to this year's Keeper, Madison Lam."

Madison beamed as she accepted the book. She caught Bailee's eye, flashing a big smile. Then she grew serious, remembering the role she was to perform. Using the bookmark as a guide, Madison opened the book. She cleared her throat and began.

"The Bellwoods is home to many stories and legends, but the one that brings us here tonight is Abigail Snook's. Many years ago, she disappeared while walking in these very woods and was never seen again. But there are some who say she isn't gone. They say she returns to the woods every Halloween, the anniversary of her disappearance. And on that night, she plays a game."

Noah shot Bailee an excited look. A hush had fallen over the crowd. Even the breeze dropped. It felt like the whole world was holding its breath, waiting to hear more.

"According to legend, only when a player rings the bell will the game end, and Abigail's spirit will be sent away for one more year," said Madison.

"But if players fail to reach the bell, Abigail will be free to terrorize the town until the next game is played," Jade added in a spooky voice.

"Three players will be chosen. And while three players will enter the woods, only one can ring the bell," Madison continued. "This person will be dubbed the winner and form part of next year's game Committee." She gestured to Arlo.

"I know who this year's winner is gonna be—me," whispered Fen from somewhere to Bailee's right. He exchanged high fives with Luca.

Bailee scowled.

"Each player *must* bring one item into the Bellwoods. This will act as their gift. Should the player be caught by the ghost of Abigail Snook, sacrificing their gift is said to ensure them safe passage out of the woods," said Madison, her voice taking on the tone of someone telling a ghost story.

"What did you bring? For your gift?" Noah whispered to Bailee.

She pulled her Bellwoods journal from her waistband.

"Your diary?" He raised an eyebrow.

"It's full of Bellwoods stories." She elbowed him playfully. "Everything I've ever heard about Abigail, the game, and the Bellwoods."

Noah eyed the journal, a hungry look in his eye now. "I'm going to need to read that. For research purposes, of course."

"Well, then, you better hope it isn't stolen by the ghost of Abigail Snook."

"Get to the good stuff!" a kid in the crowd yelled at the Committee.

"Yeah, spill it, Arlo!" Fen joined. "Is it true the ghost made your family win the lottery?"

Arlo's face glowed red. They said nothing, just scowled at the crowd, then directed their gaze to the Bellwoods, looking like they'd rather be anywhere else.

"What's Fen talking about?" Noah whispered.

"It's an old rumor about the game," Bailee said. "Legend

says, the first player who rings the bell doesn't just win bragging rights—they get a prize, too. People call it the Ghost's Gift. Abigail supposedly bestows it on anyone who can beat her at her game."

"And what do they get?" Noah asked.

"Anything they want."

Over the years, Bailee, Fen, and Madison had spent hours debating what they'd ask for if they won the Ghost's Gift. They always started with the obvious things first: money, fame, and popularity. Then they'd get creative: a puppy who never grew up. Or a box of donuts that never emptied. Or a summer vacation that never ended.

Settling on just one perfect gift had once been impossible. But if the Ghost's Gift was real, Bailee knew just what she'd ask for today—her old life back. She'd go back to a time before her dad lost his job, before her mom started working all the time, and before Nan's health scare. Before everyone at school started hating her. Bailee felt a pang of longing for her old life. As she looked around at her classmates, giggling and gossiping at the edge of the woods, her old life felt so close, like she could reach out and grab it with both hands. She knew the Ghost's Gift was just a story, same as the rest of the rumors crowding the pages of her Bellwoods journal, but she longed for it to be real.

She eyed Arlo again, thinking of how Mrs. Jackson's lottery win had come just at the right time. But life was like that, wasn't it? Sometimes things just happened. It was luck that had saved

Mrs. Jackson's bookstore. Not some magical gift from a ghost.

"Are we done with the interruptions?" Madison said, a warning note in her voice.

Fen didn't say anything more. Bailee saw him scowl.

Bailee wasn't the only one Fen was angry with after the Day of the Dare. He'd been frosty toward Madison ever since returning from his three-day suspension. He figured that since Madison had gotten detention that day too, she should also feel betrayed by Bailee, just like he did. But Madison had gone on being friends with Bailee, almost like nothing had happened. Fen felt Madison had chosen Bailee over him. And he wasn't happy about it.

Madison brushed Fen's interruption aside. "It's time to choose the players." She closed the book of Bellwoods Game rules and tucked it into the back pocket of her jeans. Jade dug around in her satchel and produced a small drawstring bag. The color was a faded charcoal gray, worn and tattered just like the book. Looking closely, Bailee saw three small stars on one side, hand-stitched in silver thread.

"Could everyone volunteering please step forward?" Madison called.

"Good luck," Noah whispered.

"You're not volunteering?" Bailee asked.

"Nah, I have other plans," said Noah cryptically.

Bailee shot him a questioning look. But Noah said nothing else.

Bailee took a deep breath. Then she stepped forward.

There were thirteen volunteers in all. Fen was among them, of course, looking smug. With one hand, he bounced a six-sided die up and down, the kind used for playing board games. Next to him stood Beth Yang, the fastest kid in class, holding a fistful of wildflowers. Erica Livingstone had volunteered too, looking more nervous than she had earlier that day in the cafeteria. Bailee noticed an old sepia-toned picture sticking out of her jacket pocket.

Fen, Beth, and Erica, competitive, athletic, and well-liked, were obvious volunteers. But a few unexpected faces had stepped forward too.

Oliver Moore, who'd once fainted at a sleepover while watching *E.T. the Extra-Terrestrial*—a movie that was totally not that scary—stood next to Erica. He trembled slightly, a large coin tucked in one clammy fist. Another surprise was Carmen Alverez. Always first with her hand in the air after a teacher's question but last picked for sports teams, Carmen looked small but self-assured among the other volunteers. She had one arm looped through the handle of a large, boxy flashlight. Her face was a mask of determination.

Jade and Madison turned their backs, fiddling with the drawstring bag for a few moments. Then they turned to face the crowd again.

"Inside this bag are thirteen stones, one for each of our volunteers," Madison announced, holding the bag up for everyone to see. "Three of those stones are marked. Each volunteer will draw one out. Those holding the marked stones will become our players."

Madison moved down the line of volunteers, holding the small well-worn bag open in front of them. One by one, each kid slipped a hand inside and drew out a stone.

"No looking until everyone has drawn," Madison warned, holding the bag out to Oliver. He took an extra-long time choosing his stone. Then, last but not least, it was Bailee's turn.

"Nice speech, Mads," Bailee whispered, fishing out the one remaining stone from the bag. She held it tightly in her palm, resisting the urge to look.

"Good luck." Madison winked at her best friend, then rejoined Jade and Arlo at the edge of the woods.

"The stones have been drawn," Madison announced. "Those holding one marked with an X will become our three players. Deal?"

There was a collective murmur of affirmation.

Bailee felt her hand growing warm around the stone clamped inside. Her nerves jangled. The moment she'd long been waiting for had arrived. In just a few seconds, she'd find out if she was a Bellwoods Game player.

"Ready?" called Madison.

A hush fell across the cemetery. No birds called, and the remaining leaves on the trees in the Bellwoods had fallen still and silent.

After what felt like an eternity, Madison's voice rang out. "Reveal!"

All around, there were cries of delight and groans of disappointment as each volunteer discovered their fate.

The first yell of excitement was Fen's. He held his marked stone aloft like a victor with a trophy. His friends crowded around him, slapping his back and cheering.

Bailee groaned. Of course Fen was chosen.

The second player turned out to be Carmen Alverez. She stared down at her own marked stone, eyes wide with shock. Classmates pressed in close, bubbling with questions and congratulations. For once, Carmen didn't know what to say. She clutched her stone, looking both pleased and uncomfortable with all the attention.

"Where's the third one?" a voice yelled.

"Who has it?" said another.

Bailee scanned the row of volunteers, searching. Everyone was craning their necks, trying to find out who the last player could be.

Then Bailee looked down at the stone in her own open hand.

It was marked with a bold letter X.

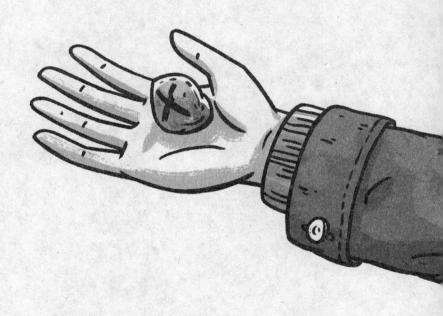

CHAPTER 7
A BAD OMEN

"**O**ur players have been chosen!" Madison announced. She gestured toward Bailee, Carmen, and Fen as if she were a game-show host introducing this week's contestants.

The players stood in a line with the Bellwoods at their backs. The rest of the kids crowded close. Trees towered overhead and cast everyone in the cemetery in cool shadow. The breeze had taken on a cold, cutting edge. Bailee bounced up and down on her toes, her stomach fluttering with a mix of excitement and nerves. This was it, what she'd been looking forward to all these years. She hugged her Bellwoods journal tightly to her chest. Just about everything that had happened the past three weeks—her falling-out with Fen, her status as an outcast at school, her parents always busy with work, and her nan's TIA—had made Bailee feel as if she'd been cursed or something. But at least she'd been picked to play the Bellwoods Game. Now all she had to do was focus on getting to the bell first.

She eyed Fen and Carmen, standing on either side. Fen looked smug and unconcerned, as usual. Carmen's expression was harder to read. She looked calm, but Bailee couldn't help but notice the way her eyes blinked and darted in all directions. Maybe Bailee wasn't the only one feeling nervous.

Madison opened her mouth to speak again, but Arlo cut her off.

"Stay together and stick to the paths if you can," they said, words coming all in a rush. "Don't trust what you see—it's not—it's not—real—Abigail—" They coughed. "Get to the bell as qui-qui-quick—" The words caught in Arlo's throat. They coughed again. "Forget—gift—just finish—finish—game." Arlo spluttered to a stop, the last bit coming out thin and strangled. They were red in the face now, hands clutching their throat as if the words had stuck there, choking them.

Jade put a reassuring hand on Arlo's shoulder, looking at them with a mixture of concern and unease. When Arlo had quieted, Jade turned to the players. "Arlo's right. People treat the game as a race, but it really doesn't matter *who* rings the bell, as long as one of you does. It's the only way to keep Fall Hollow safe for one more year." Jade's voice took on a spooky tone, like this was all part of the fun.

"Pssh," Fen scoffed under his breath. "I'm playing to win."

"Fen's definitely going to win," came a whisper at Bailee's shoulder. A glance behind showed Brendan, Luca, and Gabby with their heads together.

"Not Carmen?" said Luca in mock surprise. "She'll probably bore the ghost to death. *Did you know that being a ghost isn't scientifically possible?*" His high-pitched impression that sounded nothing like Carmen elicited laughter from the other two.

"Ghosts are already dead," said Brendan, elbowing Luca in the ribs.

"I know who I'm *not* rooting for . . . ," said Gabby, not needing to finish her thought.

Bailee felt her face grow warm. She turned her attention back to the Committee, jaw clenched. She forced herself to smile as she watched Madison and Jade talk about the lore of the game. They were saying something about times when previous players had failed to reach the bell, but she couldn't concentrate on their voices, not with her heart thumping loudly in her chest. She took a big breath in and let it out slowly, imagining her stormy thoughts growing still and calm. She redirected her mind to more pleasant thoughts, like picturing herself emerging from the woods, Bellwoods Game winner. That would shut Gabby up.

"It's time," Jade whispered in Madison's ear. She opened the book again, flipping to a specific page.

"Can our players please step forward, then line up facing the woods?" said Madison. Then she read from the book. "After the players are chosen, the beginning of the game will be marked by the ringing of the bell."

At that moment, as if in answer to Madison's words, a bell tolled from somewhere deep in the woods.

CLANG. CLANG. CLANG.

The sound made goose bumps raise up all over Bailee's arms. Fen and Carmen startled beside her. Jade and Madison whirled around to face the woods, confusion showing on their faces.

A sense of familiarity prickled at the back of Bailee's mind. She paged through her Bellwoods journal, searching for a particular passage.

ENTRY #26
HEARING THE BELL IS A
BAD OMEN

ANYONE WHO HEARS THE BELL BETTER
WATCH OUT
ABIGAIL SNOOK
WILL BE AFTER THEM!

"It's begun," said Arlo. Unlike the others, they didn't look surprised by the sound of the bell. Arlo stared at the woods, a grim, knowing look on their face. "You'll have to play. There's no turning back now. I'm sorry," they said, looking at Carmen, Fen, and Bailee.

The bell stopped. The last of its peals faded away. An uneasy hush settled at the edge of the woods.

"Nice, Mads," said Fen after a beat, smirking. "You got some kid stashed out in the woods to ring the bell on cue? Real spooky. Almost had me."

"No . . . ," said Madison, brow furrowed. "It wasn't us. Was it?" Madison turned to Jade, looking for answers. But the other girl wasn't paying attention. She was staring at the Bellwoods, a far-off look in her eyes, as if remembering something long forgotten. Beside them, Arlo put their head in their hands.

"What are you all talking about? I didn't hear any bell," Gabby said, one eyebrow raised. Murmurs of agreement rose from the crowd. "Is this part of the game or something? You all pretend something spooky is happening to scare the rest of us?"

"We're not playing pretend," said Bailee. She turned to Noah. "You heard it, didn't you? The bell was so loud. You had to have heard it."

But Noah shook his head. "I didn't hear anything." His troubled gaze shifted to the woods.

A fresh wave of goose bumps cascaded down Bailee's arms. The words from her journal rang in her head over and over again. *Bad omen, bad omen, bad omen.*

"Perhaps it was some sort of auditory group hallucination,"

said Carmen. "Brought on by the game and our heightened expectations of possible supernatural occurrences?"

"Sure," Fen said, voice heavy with sarcasm. "Or Mads and the Committee are just pranking us. You know, something a bit more realistic?"

Bailee didn't know anything about auditory hallucinations, but she did know Madison better than anyone else. Yes, organizing an elaborate plan to ring the bell for dramatic effect to start the game was totally something Madison would do. And yes, her friend was, hands down, the best actress at Beckett Elementary. But Bailee knew even Madison couldn't fake the look on her face now—could she? Bailee watched her friend's eyes dart from Jade to the woods, face clouded with suspicion and unease. No, whatever had just happened, it hadn't been part of Madison's plan for tonight.

"Whatever," said Fen. "Let's just do this thing. Can we go now or what?"

Madison turned her attention back to the book of rules, fumbling for the right page. "The—the sound of the bell marks the beginning of the game. Good luck, everyone. Fall Hollow is depending on you." She closed the book and stared at her classmates, unsure of what else to say.

No one moved or spoke.

Finally, with a shout, Fen took off at a sprint. He charged into the woods, high-stepping over rocks and dodging tree branches.

Cheers followed him.

Carmen unfroze. She jogged after Fen and, with a quick backward glance, disappeared into the woods. A few claps followed.

Bailee didn't move. She eyed the trees looming over her with distrust, nerves jangling louder than ever. She'd never believed the stories about the woods, not really. They were always just fun and games to her. But something about hearing the bell left her rattled.

"Look, she's too afraid to play," whispered Gabby.

"Better go find Principal Bright. Maybe that's why she ratted on Fen. She's scared of the woods," said Luca's mocking voice.

Bailee felt her jaw tighten as resolve sparked inside her. They could believe she was the one who told about the dare if they wanted. But she wasn't afraid. Not of the woods or anything in them.

She tucked her journal into her waistband and gave it a reassuring tap. Then she ran for the trees.

CHAPTER 8
INTO THE WOODS

Bailee leaped over fallen logs and moss-covered stones. Slick leaves slipped underfoot, and tall grass grabbed at her ankles, but she pushed on. Up ahead, she could hear Fen and Carmen crashing through the woods.

This is it. She was really playing the Bellwoods Game. The thought spurred Bailee on. She ran faster.

She followed Fen and Carmen for few minutes, then she swung right, searching.

Bailee was no stranger to the Bellwoods. She knew the system of paths that snaked through the trees almost as well as she knew the layout of her own home. Wading through the crowded underbrush might be the most direct way to the bell, but it wasn't the fastest. She'd be able to move much more quickly if she took Arlo's advice and kept to a path. All she had to do was find the right one.

To her left, the sounds of Carmen and Fen moving through the woods grew fainter and fainter. Soon, all Bailee could hear were the creak of tree trunks and her own footsteps. She walked carefully, eyes alert for any sign of a path.

Then the snap of a twig made her jump.

It came from the direction of the cemetery, behind her. Bailee paused, listening. There was another snap and the rustle of branches, like someone pushing through a thick stand of trees.

Bailee felt her nerves flutter. Someone was approaching. It couldn't be Fen or Carmen. She'd heard them move off in the other direction. Bailee put a hand to her journal, feeling its reassuring rectangular shape beneath her sweater. The stories written within were just that—stories. They couldn't be true. But now, playing the game for herself, she didn't feel so sure.

There was another rustle. Crunching sounds followed. She heard footsteps moving fast. Someone besides Fen, Carmen, and her was in the woods, and they were coming right at her.

Bailee's breath caught in her chest as the footsteps drew closer and closer.

Then there was a dull thud. Someone cursed under their breath. A familiar voice.

"Noah?" Bailee called, sagging with relief.

"Oh. Hey!" he called back.

"What are you doing here?" She moved toward the thrashing bushes and found Noah crouched next to a stump. He winced and rubbed one shin. Mud spattered the knees of his jeans, and he had a scratch on one hand.

"Well, well, well," said Bailee, hands on her hips. "Crashing the game, I see?"

Noah shot Bailee a guilty grin. "Like you said earlier, the only way to know what goes on in the woods during the game is to see for yourself, right?"

"Is there anything you won't do for a story?" Bailee helped the boy to his feet.

"I thought I'd observe quietly in the background, but it's harder getting around in here than I expected." Noah swatted at a muddy splotch on his jeans. "If only this new kid had someone to show him around," he said, giving a dramatic sigh. "You know, someone who knew *all* about the woods and the game? Where could I find someone like that?" Noah eyed her pointedly.

Bailee snorted. She didn't know whether to be exasperated or amused by his decision to follow after her. Only official players were supposed to be in the woods on Halloween night—those were the rules. She knew the Committee, especially Madison, wouldn't be impressed by the intrusion. But she also knew Noah wasn't the type to give up and go home just because of some rules. He was determined to learn everything he could about Abigail Snook, and Bailee knew she could either help or let him wander around the woods alone, potentially getting lost or hurt in the process. She didn't want that. Besides, after a few weeks of being on Beckett's least-wanted list, it was nice having someone around who didn't despise her.

"Fine. But you'd better stick close, New Kid. I've got a game to win here," she said with a grin.

Noah nodded eagerly, and together they made their way through the woods.

Minutes later they found themselves standing on a narrow path made of hard-packed earth. Sunlight peeked through the trees, warming their shoulders. Ahead, the path wound around a stand of tall, elegant birches, then disappeared.

"This way," said Bailee. They took off at a jog.

"This will take us to the bell?" Noah asked. He huffed and puffed at Bailee's elbow as they ran.

"Sort of," she said, breathing hard. "It does come to the bell eventually, after a lot of twisting and turning and doubling back. We don't have time for all that. But luckily, there's a quicker route that branches off from this path. My nan showed it to me. She calls it *the cut*."

"Like a shortcut?" said Noah.

"More like a literal 'cut.' We need to cross the river to get to the bell, but steep cliffs run along it on either side. The cut is a gap in the cliffs that will let us go right through. It's the fastest way to the bell from here, but not too many people know about it."

"So we're just telling anyone about the cut now?" came Fen's voice from off in the woods. He stepped out of the dense underbrush onto the path ahead of them.

Oh, now he'll talk to me, thought Bailee, jaw clenching. "I'm the one who showed you the cut in the first place, so I can tell whoever I want. What are you doing here anyway? I thought you'd be halfway to the bell by now."

"What am *I* doing here? What's *he* doing here?" Fen said, gesturing to Noah. "Last time I checked, there were only supposed to be *three* Bellwoods Game players."

"He's just doing some research," said Bailee, defensive. "It's not a big deal." Noah pulled his notepad and pen out of his pocket and brandished them at Fen as proof.

"Great. Tell the whole world about the game," grumbled Fen, crossing his arms. "Guess I shouldn't be surprised. You're terrible at keeping secrets." He looked hard at Bailee.

She opened her mouth to say something nasty but was interrupted by the sound of approaching footsteps. All three spun around just in time to see Carmen come into view.

She didn't see them right away. She was moving fast along

the path, shooting worried looks behind her. She yelped when she finally saw them, skidding to a halt just inches from Noah.

"Don't sneak up on me like that!" she said, hand over her heart.

"Technically, I think you snuck up on us," said Noah.

"Huh." Carmen tilted her head. "Who knew sneaking up on someone could be just as startling as being snuck up on?"

"How did you get behind us?" Bailee asked, directing her attention to Carmen.

"I . . . um . . . I'm not sure," said Carmen, blinking fast. She shot another uneasy look behind her. "I memorized a map of the woods ages ago, but navigating the paths is more difficult in practice, I suppose. I'm looking for that path through the cliffs. The one that takes you to the river?"

"Great. Everyone knows about the cut now." Fen threw his hands up. "Well," he said, looking at them all exasperatedly, "let's get going. The sooner we finish this game, the sooner I can go collect free candy."

"You're coming with us?" said Bailee, raising an eyebrow.

"What am I going to do? Walk five steps ahead of everyone the whole way?"

"Arlo did say we should stick together," said Carmen.

"Sure," Fen said. "But don't think I'm waiting around for all of you when we get close to the bell. I don't know if a ghost really made Arlo's mom win the lottery, but I'm going to be the one ringing that bell, just in case."

Bailee rolled her eyes. "Whatever you say, Fen."

They hurried along the path single file. Fen jogged ahead, impatient, while Bailee, Noah, and Carmen stuck closer together.

"So, Bailee," said Noah. "Tell me some of the stories in your journal. Ones about Abigail and the game."

Bailee's hand went to her waistband. She felt the reassuring rectangular shape of her notebook tucked there, safe and sound. "They're mostly rumors I've heard over the years. Things like

'So-and-so's friend saw a shadowy figure standing on top of the ridge by the falls.' Or 'Someone's sister swears Abigail Snook tripped her while out walking in the woods one night.' Stuff like that," she replied.

"Spooky," said Noah.

"More like boring," called Fen from up ahead. "That's all basic horror stuff. Jump-scares or people too embarrassed to admit they spooked themselves out in the woods. That's the whole reason Halloween was invented—to scare people."

"Actually, the origins of Halloween can be traced back to ancient times," said Carmen, jogging along behind Noah. "It was once known as All Hallows' Eve, a day when the boundaries separating this world and the next were said to be thin. People say it's a time when ghosts and spirits visit the realm of the living. People would celebrate with bonfires and dress up in scary costumes, hoping to scare away these spirits. The ancient Celts called the day Samhain."

"Sow-wane?" said Fen, arching an eyebrow.

"It's kind of like a harvest festival, right?" Noah chimed in. "I was reading an article about it the other day."

"Sort of." Carmen nodded. "Many cultures see it as a day of remembrance and celebration of departed loved ones. In Mexico, celebrations are held at the beginning of November. They call it Día de los Muertos—Day of the Dead."

"Thanks for the info dump," Fen grumbled.

"If you've got better stories, let's hear 'em," Noah called after the other boy.

Fen slowed, letting the others catch up. "Yeah, I've got some stories. New Kid, you ever heard of Ben Bradley? He also disappeared in the woods years ago, not long after Abigail Snook did. But no one talks about him. Some say Abigail's ghost got him, but others think he was snatched up by some stranger. His family didn't make a stink about it, though. Told the police he ran away. Then his whole family left town."

Bailee made a face. "You just made that up. I've never heard of anyone named Ben Bradley. And anyway, what kind of parents would just move away and not even look for their missing kid?"

"Maybe they hated him," argued Fen. "Maybe they were glad he was gone. See, that's a real scary story right there. Not some bogeyman or wailing spirit out in the woods. Just a crummy real-life family." Fen kicked at a pinecone, sending it skittering into the brush.

"The scariest part is that there are people who would fall for stories like that." Bailee sniffed. Fen scowled in return.

"Instances of child abductions by strangers, though terrible, are actually quite rare, despite being heavily featured in the news," Carmen said thoughtfully. "In such cases, families are often the first to be investigated."

"See! Even the walking search engine agrees with me," said Fen. He quickened his pace, leaving them behind.

Bailee was about to point out that Carmen wasn't exactly agreeing with him when she saw Fen pause. He looked frozen, as still as the trees all around them.

"What's wrong?" Noah asked.

"I thought I heard something . . . ," Fen whispered.

They all halted, listening. Leaves drifted to the ground around them. They strained to hear anything out of the ordinary.

Suddenly Fen pointed at something in the distance. "What the . . . ?"

Bailee followed his gaze. But she saw nothing.

"What the—*what*?" Noah said skeptically.

Fen didn't reply, just stared off into the gloom of the woods. Then he yelled. "There it is again! Up there! Do you see it?" Fen took off, bounding up the path like a hound after a hare. He disappeared around a bend.

"Fen! Wait!" Bailee called. But it was too late. He vanished from sight.

CHAPTER 9
OTHER HAUNTINGS

Fear tingled in Bailee's fingertips. Something wasn't right.

All three sprinted after Fen.

"I didn't see anything. Did either of you?" Noah puffed as they ran.

Carmen and Bailee shook their heads. If Fen had seen something, it had only been visible to him.

"Look! There," called Carmen as they climbed a small hill. They skidded to a stop. Ahead, Fen stood with his back to them, as still as a statue.

Fen didn't acknowledge them when they arrived. He swayed gently on his feet, as if caught in an invisible storm.

"Fen?" said Bailee. She meant to sound annoyed, but the question came out small.

"Do you see it?" Fen said. His voice was flat and emotionless. He lifted a hand and pointed to something ahead of him. Something neither Bailee, Carmen, nor Noah could see.

"What's happening?" Carmen whispered.

"I don't know," Bailee whispered back.

"I see . . . I see . . . ," Fen began.

"What? What is it?" Bailee said, voice stretched thin.

Fen didn't speak for a moment. He turned toward them slowly. He fixed his gaze on them, staring wide-eyed, as if paralyzed by fright.

"Fen, stop. This—this isn't funny," said Bailee, trying to sound firm.

"You don't understand," he whispered. *"You don't see what I see."*

"What? What do you see?" Noah asked, voice almost pleading now.

Fen continued to stare, his expression growing more and more fearful.

He jumped into the air and let out a howl. He drew his hands up to his ears, fingers contracted like claws. His face contorted into a wicked grin. He held the pose for a beat, then doubled over with laughter.

Bailee, Noah, and Carmen groaned.

"One ghost in the woods isn't enough for you? You need to invent another?" said Bailee with as much disdain as she could muster. "C'mon, let's get to the bell. Leave Fen to his imaginary friends." She pushed past the boy. Noah and Carmen followed.

"Yeah, if we hurry, Bailee can get home in time to tattle on us all for being in the woods. She's good at that," said Fen, stomping along the path behind them.

Bailee tensed but didn't look back. "Leave it alone, Fen."

"What? You've gone into the woods during school hours *plenty* of times. But suddenly, when someone else does it, you go running to a teacher and get everyone in trouble? Why? I just don't get it."

Bailee whirled to face him, fists clenched at her sides. "How many times do I have to tell you? It wasn't me who told about the dare."

"Gabby *saw you* with Bright right before we got busted," said Fen accusingly. "Other kids did too. Then you conveniently disappeared for the rest of the day. You were the only one who didn't show up at the falls and the only one who didn't get detention."

"*One* of the only people, actually," Carmen added. She didn't have a phone and hadn't received the message about the dare. Nor had anyone thought to invite her along.

Bailee shook her head in frustration. She'd tried to tell Fen where she'd been that day. She'd marched right up to him after he'd returned from his detention, determined to set the record straight. But, surrounded by the angry and mistrustful stares of their classmates, the words had tangled on her tongue. Images of Nan, alone and small against that hospital bed, crowded in, squeezing Bailee's throat tight. The story of what had happened that day, the real one, was too painful—too private. Besides, she'd told herself, she hadn't done anything wrong. She didn't owe anyone an explanation.

"If it wasn't you, who else could it have been?" Fen demanded.

"I don't know. But it *wasn't me*. And your going around telling people it was doesn't make it true." She stared hard at Fen, willing herself not to flinch.

He didn't speak for a moment. "Whatever," he replied finally. "I'm heading to the bell. Maybe when I win, I'll ask Abigail Snook for better friends."

He pushed past Bailee and stormed up the path, disappearing into the trees.

No one spoke for a long moment. Carmen and Noah exchanged uneasy glances. Bailee clenched and unclenched her jaw, waiting for her anger and hurt to subside.

"C'mon. Let's get going," she said after a long pause. She and Noah started walking up the path, following Fen. Then Bailee stopped and turned around.

Carmen hadn't moved. She looked rooted to the path, an uncertain expression on her face.

"Carmen? Aren't you coming with us?" Bailee asked.

"Oh," said Carmen quickly. "I wasn't sure if . . . I didn't know . . . I mean, yes. I'll come. I'd like that."

She jogged to catch up. They walked along the path together in silence.

Bailee considered telling Noah and Carmen about everything that happened on the Day of the Dare. They would understand, wouldn't they? They'd listen. But as Bailee started to speak, she felt her mouth go dry and her heart begin to race.

No. She wasn't ready.

"You know," said Noah, squeezing beside her on the

narrow path. "This is a pretty nice walk. Peaceful. Now that Fen's gone."

Bailee snorted. Then she asked the question she'd been wondering about since this afternoon. "Why don't you hate me like the others? You got detention on the Day of the Dare too."

"Hey, I knew we weren't allowed in the woods during school hours, but I went in anyway. Besides, if you say you didn't tell Bright, I believe you."

"Why? No one else does."

Noah sighed and hunched his shoulders. "Let's just say, I know what it feels like. Everyone talking about you but no one talking *to* you. Being both the center of attention and invisible at the same time. And I definitely know what it's like, having people say stuff about me that wasn't true."

Bailee studied Noah. The boy's usual ease had vanished, replaced by a glum, faraway look, like he was thinking back to a time he'd rather forget.

"Do you want to talk about it?" she asked.

Noah was quiet for another moment. He sighed again. "We had a student paper at my old school. I used to write for it. Lots of students did. It was a blast. Until my last article."

"Okay . . ."

"It ran in the final issue of the year, right before summer vacation. Right before my family and I were all set to move here so my mom could start her new practice. The article I wrote— it was kind of intense, probably the best one I ever worked on. I found out some stuff about the guy my old school was named after, Edgar T. Howard. I won't go into all the details, but turns out he wasn't a good guy. Like, *not at all*. I thought it would make a good story. So did the paper's faculty advisor. He fact-checked my article and everything. It was all true. So we published the story."

"Then what happened?" Bailee asked.

"People found the article . . . upsetting. But not in the way I expected."

"Let me guess—they got mad at you. Not that Howard guy," said Bailee.

Noah nodded. "I guess some people thought I was attacking our school or saying it was a bad place or something. But that wasn't what the article was about at all. Our school was great, but the guy it was named after wasn't. I just thought people should know. And if they did, maybe we could change things for the better." Noah kicked at a rock. "But people just got mad. It was a rough last few weeks of school. People I thought were my friends stopped talking to me. I heard my name whispered in the halls all the time. I even heard that parents called into the school and complained about how the stuff in my article was *inappropriate*. But I was just writing about stuff that had really happened. How could writing the truth be inappropriate?"

Bailee frowned and shook her head. Some adults always managed to find ways to be disappointing.

"Anyway," Noah continued. "School ended after all that

happened, and my family and I packed up and moved here. Hardly any of my old friends have talked to me since. Most haven't answered any of my messages or asked about my move or my new school. It feels like they've forgotten all about me."

Bailee shook her head. "I'm sorry, Noah. That's rough."

"Thanks. But it's not a big deal." His voice was suddenly cool and detached. He pulled out his pen and notepad and flipped absently through the pages. "Just a hazard of the job. I've learned that sometimes people aren't going to like what they read, especially when it's the truth."

"I—"

But Bailee was interrupted.

There was a yell from behind them, somewhere off in the woods. It was a familiar voice, one they now realized had been far too quiet during Noah's story.

"Oh no," said Noah, looking around.

Bailee looked around too. They were all alone on the path.

Carmen was gone.

CHAPTER 10
A FLICKER OF LIGHT

Bailee and Noah froze.

"Carmen!" Noah yelled.

Bailee's eyes moved over the woods, searching. Had that yell really belonged to Carmen? How long had she been gone before they'd noticed?

"Is it possible she's hiding? Joking around, like Fen did?" said Noah, a hopeful note in his voice.

"I don't think she's much of a joker. Not like that," said Bailee, a sinking feeling in her stomach.

"Or the older kids? Maybe it's all a prank, set up by Jade and Arlo?"

Bailee hadn't considered this. It was possible, yes. But something told her this also wasn't true. She thought back to the beginning of the game and the look of genuine surprise on Jade's face when she heard the bell. And how Arlo had been acting so strange, so unlike themself. No, this didn't feel like a setup. Something else was going on.

There was another strangled cry, clearer this time. A call for help. It was definitely Carmen.

Bailee and Noah took off, sprinting back down the path the way they had come.

"Carmen! Keep yelling so we can find you!" called Bailee. She swallowed hard, trying to ignore the knot of guilt pulling tight in her stomach. Arlo had told them to stick together, but only minutes after the game started, she'd fought with Fen, and they were all split up. Now Carmen might be hurt or something. Maybe Gabby was right, Bailee thought. Maybe she did ruin everything.

They climbed a small hill, then followed the path as it swung to their right. Suddenly a figure loomed up in front of them. Bailee skidded to a stop. Noah nearly smacked into her.

A girl stood before them, someone they didn't recognize. She stood in the shadows, little more than a sil- houette in the low light.

"Someone needs help. Back there," she said, pointing off the path, into the woods.

As if on cue, they heard Carmen call again. "HELP!"

They shot one last look at the girl, then darted toward Carmen's voice, pushing into the dense underbrush. Leaves crunched and twigs snapped underfoot. Bailee winced as a branch caught the back of her hand, leaving a long, thin scratch.

"Do you see her?" Noah gasped, ducking under a low-hanging branch.

Bailee shook her head, eyes searching. Another yell came from off to their right.

"There!" shouted Noah.

In the distance was a flicker of light. It bounced and bobbed, swinging wildly. It was Carmen, flashlight in hand, standing in the shadows near the base of a high, rocky cliff. As they drew closer, they saw Carmen bent in an awkward position. Her arms flailed as if she were struggling against an invisible attacker.

"Carmen!" Bailee puffed, rushing to the girl's side.

"Are you hurt? What's wrong?" said Noah, wheezing. He bent over with his hands on his knees.

"It's my foot," whispered Carmen. Her eyes flicked downward.

Bailee and Noah followed her gaze and saw that one of her legs was sunk, knee-deep, in a narrow crevice. They watched as she wrenched her leg this way and that, but her foot stuck fast.

"We thought you were right behind us on the path. How did you get way out here?" said Noah. He and Bailee grabbed hold of Carmen's arms and started to pull.

"I stopped to tie one of my bootlaces. When I looked up, you two were gone." Carmen's words came in a hushed, hurried jumble. "I ran along the path, expecting to catch up. But the path became harder and harder to make out. Soon there was no path at all. It just vanished. That's when, well . . ." Carmen gestured at her foot.

"It's really stuck." Noah frowned, sitting back on his heels.

Carmen nodded, struggling. She shot a wary look at the cliff looming over them.

"Don't panic. I think I can get my hand in there. I'll untie your laces, and then you can pull your foot free," said Bailee.

"Okay. But hurry. I—I don't think it's safe here," Carmen whispered, eyes locked on the cliff.

"Why? What is it?" Noah got to his feet and followed Carmen's gaze. Just discernible in the gloom was a small opening in the cliff face—a cave.

"I—I think there's something in there." Carmen's voice wavered. "I heard . . . whispering." Carmen struggled again, blinking furiously at the gaping mouth of the cave.

Bailee felt goose bumps prick up along her arms. Carmen never broke a sweat during Ms. Chivers's brutal pop quizzes. She never looked fazed by the teasing comments classmates threw her way. But now the girl was rattled.

Bailee shot a suspicious look at the cave, then knelt on her hands and knees beside Carmen's stuck foot. She pushed up her sleeves, then snaked her hand down inside the crevice, fingers searching for Carmen's laces. She grimaced, imagining all the creatures hidden within, but she pushed the thoughts away. She needed to focus.

"It's probably just the wind, those sounds you heard," Noah said in his best reassuring voice.

"I don't think so," said Carmen, her eyes fixed on the mouth of the cave. "It sounded like someone talking. I know how this sounds, but—it sounded like someone calling my name."

"For real?" Noah studied the cave with real mistrust now. He inched toward it, listening.

"It's probably just your imagination. The game's got us all worked up," said Bailee. Still, she felt her legs begin to shake. She urged her fingers to move faster as they found Carmen's bootlace and started working the knot.

"That's what I assumed too, at first. But a voice was saying my name, I swear. It got louder and louder. Then I thought I saw something moving around in there. I turned my flashlight on to see better. But there was nothing."

"Actually, I think I hear something too," Noah said uneasily. He inched closer to the cliff.

Carmen fumbled with her flashlight, training it on the mouth of the cave. She jerked her leg, struggling against the crevice's grip.

"Hold on, I think I've almost got it," said Bailee, working the laces as fast as she could. Just a few more tugs.

With a pop, Carmen's foot slid free. Bailee grabbed hold of the now-empty boot, careful not to lose it to the murky depths below. She wiggled it out of the crevice and handed it back to Carmen, who was teetering on one foot.

"Thanks, Bailee." Carmen's voice was heavy with relief. She flicked off her flashlight and set it on the ground, then jammed her foot inside the boot. She cinched the laces tight, all the while keeping her eyes fixed on the cave.

"Uh, the sound is getting louder," Noah said. He leaned

toward the cliff as if his feet were unwilling to go any farther, but his curiosity left him unable to look away.

Carmen made a small noise in her throat. She picked up her flashlight and held it before her like a weapon, ready to strike.

Bailee heard it now too. The whispering. It was more of a rustling really, but building, growing louder and louder. Soon the sound had grown to a dull roar. Like something, or *quite a few somethings*, coming toward them—fast. Suddenly, like a light bulb switching on, Bailee knew what was about to happen. She opened her mouth to tell Noah to duck. But not in time.

"BATS!" Noah yelped. He dropped to the ground.

Bailee and Carmen crouched and put their arms over their heads as hundreds of bats streamed out of the cave. But instead of flying up into the sky like they should have done, they descended upon Bailee, Carmen, and Noah, swarming around them like a living cloud.

"This isn't right! Bats don't attack people like this!" Carmen yelled.

Bailee opened her mouth to agree but clamped it shut instead. Tiny claws plucked at her hair and jacket. She fought the urge to run. She scrunched her eyes closed and tucked her chin to her chest, waving her arms around to fend off the flurry of small bodies and furiously flapping wings. She felt them nip at her fingers and their little bodies crashing into her over and over again.

Finally Bailee couldn't take any more.

She ran. She bolted away from the cave, arms flailing. The cloud of bats followed. The ones around Carmen and Noah did too. They followed Bailee as she tore through the woods, jumping over logs and bushes. She reached a bright clearing where blue sky peered down on her from between the trees above. She stumbled over a rock and fell to her hands and knees. She put her arms over her head again, bracing for another attack.

But nothing happened.

She raised her head.

The bats flapped around the perimeter of the clearing like the swirling winds of a hurricane. Bailee felt as if she was in the eye of a storm. The bats did a lap around the clearing, and another. Then, as if frustrated by something, the bats suddenly streamed away. They disappeared into the trees, a twining, twisting ribbon of tiny bodies and wings. Then they were gone.

Bailee lay still. She waited, tense and listening. Finally she uncurled. There was no sign of the bats.

"What. ON EARTH. Just happened?" said Noah. He and Carmen joined Bailee in the clearing. Noah extended a hand, helping Bailee to her feet.

"I don't know," said Carmen, pale with disbelief. Bailee was pretty sure it was the first time Carmen had said such a thing. Carmen always knew everything.

"Come on," Bailee said after a long moment. "Let's find the path again." She brushed dirt and clinging leaves from the knees of her jeans. She felt for her journal, worried she'd lost it during the confusion. But it was still tucked snug in her waistband. She let out a heavy breath of relief.

"I don't understand," Carmen said as they walked, navigating their way back to the path. "Bats in the woods makes sense. But it's still light out, too early for feeding. And they shouldn't have made those whispering sounds. Their flight and echolocation are silent, at least to human ears. They wouldn't have swarmed around us either; bats are only interested in insects. These were more like—"

"A bad horror-movie version of bats?" Bailee offered.

"I don't really watch movies." Carmen shrugged. "Though I do enjoy the occasional documentary."

Noah jotted down notes as they walked. "Whatever just happened, looks like they're all gone. For now."

"I'm certain I heard a person whispering my name before.

But it stopped after I turned my flashlight on." Carmen studied the boxy device in her hand, a thoughtful look on her face. "Something very strange is going on."

"At least it was only bats. Not the ghost of Abigail Snook," Noah said with a weak grin.

Bailee said nothing. She agreed with Carmen. Bats shouldn't have behaved like that. And how had Carmen strayed so far from the path to begin with? They had only lost track of her for a moment or two. Nothing about what had just happened made sense.

"I haven't heard the bell. There's a chance Fen hasn't gotten there yet," Bailee said, putting her worries away. "Let's finish this game and leave. I don't want to be wandering around in here after dark."

Noah nodded. Carmen looked up at the sky where the warm October sunlight had already begun to fade. She nodded too.

Together they worked their way through the woods, back toward the path.

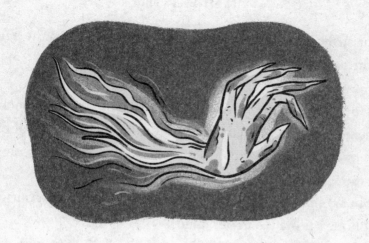

CHAPTER 11
RUN!

"**W**ho was that girl back there?" Noah whispered to Bailee as they picked their way through the underbrush.

"My name's Carmen," said Carmen.

Noah laughed. "I know who you are, Carmen Alverez, smartest kid at Beckett Elementary. You even skipped a grade, if my sources are correct?"

"Um . . . that's right." She nodded. "Went from second to fourth."

"I'm talking about the other girl Bailee and I saw, before we found you. I know I'm the new kid, but I thought I could at least recognize everyone in our grade. But there was something familiar about her, like I've seen her somewhere before. . . ."

Bailee frowned. After all the commotion with Carmen and

the bats, she had almost forgotten about the girl from the path. "I don't know who she was either."

"Maybe she's new?" Carmen suggested.

"I doubt it," Bailee replied. She reached into her back pocket for her phone. She wanted to text Madison, tell her friend about everything that had happened in the woods so far—the strange girl, the bats, her fight with Fen.

But no matter how many times she pushed the on button, her phone sat lifeless in her hand.

"What's wrong?" Noah asked, noticing Bailee's frown.

"I think my phone's dead," she replied. She pushed the power button, then all the buttons. Nothing worked.

Noah pulled out his own phone, fiddled with it, and then also frowned. "Weird. I charged mine before I came to the game. No way the battery could be dead already."

"I don't have a phone," said Carmen. "My dad says they delay brain development, and I should wait until—"

"You did a presentation for the class all about it, Carmen," said Bailee.

"Oh right," said Carmen.

"I just wish we had a way to call for help. If we need it. You know, if one of us sprains an ankle . . ." *Or we see the ghost.* The thought came unbidden. Bailee's hand went to the waist of her jeans, feeling for her journal. Her gift was there, safe and sound. Not that she believed the stories, of course. But the solidness of her journal felt reassuring all the same.

"What did that girl look like?" asked Carmen.

"I didn't get a good look," Bailee answered, preoccupied with her phone. "Did you, Noah?"

But Noah didn't say anything.

"Noah?" Bailee turned. Noah's eyes were wide and staring, fixed on something far off in the woods.

"N-n-no. But I'm pretty sure that's not her," he whispered.

Bailee followed his gaze.

In the distance was a hooded figure. It stood silent and still, hard to distinguish from the trees and shifting shadows of the woods. But it was there. And it was watching them.

"Who is that?" asked Carmen, her voice barely a whisper. She hugged her flashlight to her chest.

Impossibly, as if the figure had heard, it raised a hand, waving. Then was still. Watching.

Bailee shivered and felt fear tingle in her fingertips again. *Who is this? What is going on?*

"Are you here to play my game?" came a voice.

They jumped. The figure hadn't moved, but the voice sounded as if it had come from right beside them. An inhuman voice, the sound of a cold wind whistling through bare branches.

"Oh, I do not like that," said Carmen after a beat.

"Is this some sort of joke?" asked Noah, voice edged with fear.

"Could be," said the voice again. "I like jokes."

Bailee felt goose bumps rise on her arms and neck. Beside her, Carmen made a small noise.

"But I like stories better than jokes," continued the voice. "Will you tell me a story? Most who play the game give me one . . . eventually."

"This can't be happening. It can't be," Noah murmured to himself. He turned to Bailee and Carmen. "The ghost of Abigail Snook isn't real, right? *It can't be real.*"

"Oh, I'm real," said the voice. "You'll see."

They gasped. The figure broke into a run, crashing through the underbrush toward them. A strange wind blew all around, tossing up leaves in its wake. It was coming at them fast.

"What the—" Bailee started. But her voice was drowned out by a shriek of manic laughter.

Bailee knew she should run, but her brain felt numb, unable

to process what she was seeing. Her hand went to her journal, suddenly reminded of one of the stories she had written inside, one she'd heard long ago.

It had been a rainy day. Two students from an older grade sat with Bailee's class while they spent recess indoors. They told stories to the restless fourth graders. One told about the time his brother supposedly played the Bellwoods Game.

"What did she look like? Abigail's ghost?" one of Bailee's classmates, Ivy Stone, had asked, wide-eyed.

"He said he never saw her face. She moved too quickly," the lunch monitor said. "All he remembers is that she moved like a storm. All winds and wailing. He said his mind's a blank after that."

The story had given Bailee goose bumps back then. Now, watching the strange figure advance on them, Bailee had goose bumps again. But unfolding before her wasn't a rainy-day story; this was real life. This was happening.

Bailee's thoughts were interrupted by a voice. "Follow me! Quick!"

A girl had appeared beside Bailee, the same one she and Noah had met earlier on the path. The girl was pale with a freckled face. Her gray eyes were fixed on the approaching figure, wide with fear.

"We need to run! Now!" She gestured for Bailee, Noah, and Carmen to follow, then took off, disappearing behind a cluster of pines.

They looked at one another, then at the frightening figure sprinting toward them. They darted after the girl.

"What is that *thing* chasing us?" yelled Noah as they ran.

"I don't know," Bailee called back.

"I *really* don't want to find out!" shouted Carmen.

Branches tore at their faces and clothing. There was another shriek, so loud, the forest around them shook.

Bailee knew she shouldn't look back. Characters in her horror novels were always doing foolish stuff like that, looking behind them when they should be concentrating on getting away. But with a real-life horror story playing out in front of her, she understood the impulse. She looked back.

The cloaked figure was gaining on them, winds swirling all around. Its hood hid its face from view, but from within, two eyes glowed like green, glittering lights.

"Oof!" Bailee cried as a low branch caught her on the shoulder. She went tumbling to her hands and knees.

Carmen stopped, doubled back, and extended a hand to Bailee, who struggled to her feet again. They kept running.

"Hurry!" yelled Noah from up ahead. He stood next to the freckled girl beside an enormous fallen tree. Roots jutted out from the base of it at all angles. It looked as if it had been pushed over by a giant.

Bailee watched as the girl ducked down and disappeared from view. Noah followed. When Bailee and Carmen arrived at the tree, the other two were nowhere to be found.

"Where—" Bailee started. Then Noah's hand appeared, poking out from a small gap beneath the tree, one Bailee was sure hadn't been there a moment before. She peered inside and discovered a hollowed-out trench in the damp earth below. Noah and the girl were already crouched within. They beckoned frantically for Carmen and Bailee to join them.

In the distance there was another horrifying wail.

Bailee knelt and yanked Carmen down with her. Both dove into the hole beneath the fallen tree.

"Come out, come out!" said the figure, its voice like branches scraping on a windowpane.

From their hiding place, Bailee, Carmen, and Noah heard the wind outside pick up. All around them, trees thrashed and creaked. Branches and leaves rained down on the trunk of the tree above them.

"Stay quiet," said the freckled girl. "If it can't find us, it'll go away."

Bailee pulled her knees more tightly to her chest. There was barely enough room for all of them in the trench, but she pushed herself as far from the narrow opening as she could. She squeezed her eyes shut, wishing she were anywhere else. A memory of playing hide-and-seek as a child came to her. She used to shut her eyes, thinking that if she couldn't see her pursuers, they couldn't see her, either. But, of course, this had never saved her from getting caught. And it wouldn't save her now.

"Hello," came a voice.

Bailee cracked one eye open and gasped.

A ghostly hand reached through the narrow opening, a hand like nothing Bailee had ever seen.

Pale, long fingers, almost transparent, moved over one another like restless snakes. They stretched toward her, searching.

Bailee felt a scream build in her throat and clamped her mouth shut against it. They scrambled away from the horrific sight. Noah grabbed Carmen's shoulders, hauling her back.

"Don't let it touch you!" ordered the freckled girl.

But this was easier said than done. The hand continued to stretch toward Bailee, fingers twitching eagerly.

"Come on," said the horrible voice. "It's no fun when you hide. I like it better when you run. But if that's how you want to play . . ." The hand reared back, like a viper, ready to strike. It took aim at Bailee.

"No!" the girl cried. She threw an arm in front of the ghostly hand just as it sprang at Bailee.

At the hand's touch, the girl went limp. She collapsed at Bailee's feet, eyes going wide, her face stretched in terror.

Outside, the unearthly voice shrieked with glee. "Gotcha! But you aren't the one I'm looking for."

The hand reached for Bailee again. She flattened herself against the dirt wall of their hiding place, but there was nowhere to go. She watched in horror as the hand drifted toward her, looking more like tendrils of smoke than flesh and bone.

"You have something for me, and I want it. NOW!"

Bailee braced herself.

Then light lit the space beneath the tree.

With a shriek, the hand retreated, writhing away from the glare. It dissolved, vanishing like mist against the morning sun.

Outside their hiding place, the swirling, howling wind died. Leaves floated all around, settling back down on the ground. Then all was quiet.

"Fascinating," Carmen whispered after a long silence.

Bailee exhaled slowly. Beside her, Carmen held her flashlight like a shield. The glow illuminated their hiding place beneath the tree, all damp earth, roots, and stones. The freckled girl lay at Bailee's feet, unmoving.

Suddenly Noah made a gagging noise. "There's a spider in here!" He jostled against Carmen and Bailee, scrambling for the opening.

"Wait! Let me make sure the—*whatever that was*—is gone." Bailee poked her head out of their hiding space.

All around them, the woods were quiet and still. They were alone.

The freckled girl began to stir. Together Carmen, Bailee, and Noah helped her crawl out from under the fallen tree.

"What just happened?" Noah demanded, brushing dirt from his jeans. "Who was that? What is going on?"

The freckled girl murmured something. Carmen helped her sit up. "How did you know to do that?" she asked finally. She pointed to Carmen's flashlight.

Carmen blinked several times. "Um . . . a guess? I was sure I saw something in the cave earlier, before the strange bats attacked us. But it disappeared after I turned my flashlight on. I wondered if there was a correlation."

"That was a seriously well-timed brain wave," said Bailee. "Good job, Carmen."

Carmen's cheeks went red, but she smiled. She patted her flashlight, then looped her arm through the handle.

"This is promising," said the freckled girl. She got to her feet, swaying a bit. "Very promising." Then, without a backward glance, she walked, unsteadily, into the forest.

Bailee, Noah, and Carmen stared blankly at one another.

"Um, hello?" called Bailee. She rushed after the girl. Noah and Carmen followed.

"Oh yes. Keep up!" the girl called behind her. She was more alert now, recovering from the effects of the ghostly hand's touch. "We've got a ways to go to the bell. And we'll have to hurry. It'll be back soon."

"Who *is* this person?" asked Noah, gesturing to the girl.

Bailee shook her head. She had no idea. But whoever she was, she spoke as if she knew what was going on.

"Excuse me!" called Carmen, running to keep up. "What's promising?"

"The game, of course! The Specter has very few weaknesses; it's always learning and changing. But it hates the light. Can't deal. Smart to bring a flashlight with you."

Bailee and Noah looked at Carmen.

"It just seemed practical." She shrugged.

Ahead the freckled girl had stopped walking. She put a hand to her temple. "Wait, what was I doing?" She turned, staring at them with a puzzled look on her face.

"We don't know . . . ," said Noah, shooting Carmen and Bailee a look of disbelief.

"Oh . . . right." The girl began crisscrossing through the woods, pushing her way around a cluster of shaggy cedars. She leaped over a mucky patch, searching as she went.

"Wait!" called Bailee, annoyance replacing her earlier fear. Something very strange was going on, and this girl obviously knew more than she was telling. "What is going on? Who are you?"

"Ah, here we are." The girl bent to retrieve something from behind a large tree stump. She shook it, sending crisp leaves fluttering. Then she slung it around her shoulders—a red cloak. She whirled to face Bailee, Noah, and Carmen.

"Don't you know?" she replied. "I'm Abigail Snook."

CHAPTER 12
SNOOK AND THE SPECTER

No one spoke.

Finally Noah turned to Carmen and Bailee. "Am I *missing* something?"

They didn't reply. They were too busy gaping at the girl before them.

"You *are* her," Carmen managed after a long silence. "I've seen you before. A picture, anyway. In an old newspaper article I came across. It was about the night you disappeared."

"Holy smokes, you're right!" said Noah, clapping a hand to his forehead. "That's why she looked familiar before. I must have seen the same article in the library's archive. But how— *how is this possible?*"

"I should have recognized you right away," Carmen said.

"But I suppose no one really *expects* to run into a person who's . . ." Carmen went quiet, looking uncomfortable.

"Dead?" said Abigail in a helpful tone.

"Yes . . . Sorry," said Carmen.

"That's okay. I am dead." Abigail shrugged. Then she turned and marched off into the woods.

"Okay. She has got to stop doing that." Noah jogged after the girl, with Carmen close behind.

Bailee drifted along in their wake as if in a trance. Her fingers were numb, and her stomach felt all hollowed out and wrong. She wanted to say something, but no words came. It felt as if her mind had shut down, just closed up shop and went home for the day. Nothing made sense anymore because she'd just discovered *that ghosts were real*. Which was impossible. It was *supposed* to be impossible. Sure, she'd been collecting stories about the ghost of Abigail Snook since she was little. But they were just stories. They weren't supposed to be true.

"This is wild. You're really a ghost?" Noah was saying. He stared at Abigail as if he couldn't believe those words had actually come out of his mouth.

"Looks that way," she replied.

Bailee's eyes followed Abigail's feet, branches and leaves crunching beneath them. "But you're so . . . solid," she murmured.

Abigail looked down at her hands. "Oh, I'm not usually like this," she said, almost apologetically.

"What—what are you usually like?" asked Carmen.

"More like . . . energy," said Abigail thoughtfully. "Not really *here* enough for this world. Not *there* enough for the next."

"Other . . . *worlds*? This is . . ." Noah shook his head. He pulled out his pen and notepad and began scribbling away. Even the shock from discovering a real ghost couldn't distract him from his research.

"Normally I can only look like this if I *really* concentrate." Abigail looked down at herself. "And I can only hold my form for a moment or two. But it's different the day of the game. I become more *here*. More real. Almost like my old self, before . . . well, you know." Abigail's eyes grew distant.

"So help me understand. If *you're* Abigail," began Noah, "then what the heck was that *thing* back there that tried to attack us? It had a cloak like yours, but it looked . . . weird."

"The Specter may look like me, but we're nothing alike." Abigail's expression hardened.

"The Specter?" Bailee asked, brows knitting together. She thought she knew everything about the game, but this was different. But then again, so was the fact that Abigail's ghost was *real* and not just a town legend. This whole night was turning out to be much stranger than she'd expected.

"That's what I call it. I've never stuck around long enough to ask its *real* name, if it even has one. We don't exactly hang out," said Abigail with a shudder.

"What *is* it?" asked Carmen.

"The Specter's history is older and more complicated than anyone knows. It's not really a being. . . . It's more like a feeling. Or maybe a concept. I'm not sure. All I can tell you is, it's not a ghost like me; it's from somewhere else entirely. Does that explain it?"

"It does not," said Carmen, shaking her head.

Abigail continued, fumbling for the right words. "The Specter is like . . . an apparition. A figment of the imagination or a nightmare made real. It looks like what you expect to see."

Noah tapped his chin with his pen. "Looks like what we

expect to see . . . So because we heard stories about the creepy ghost of Abigail Snook haunting the woods . . . ?"

"Then that's what you found," Abigail finished.

"And those bats we saw," added Carmen. "That's why they were so strange, isn't it? They weren't real bats at all. . . ."

"Just one of the Specter's tricks," Abigail confirmed. "The Specter's purpose is to scare. It's all part of the game. I'll explain more, but we have to move. The Specter needs some time to recover after an attack, but it'll be back soon."

They picked up the pace. Noah and Carmen peppered the

ghostly girl with questions. Bailee drifted along behind in a daze. She took her journal from her waistband and flipped through the pages as she walked. Everything she knew about the Bellwoods Game was written inside, every rumor, every snippet of story. But there wasn't one mention of a Specter. Or the real Abigail Snook, either. Her stomach lurched. Everything she knew about the game was wrong. Well, not wrong exactly, but not quite right. Yes, the ghost of Abigail Snook really *did* haunt the woods, and there really *was* something stalking the kids of Fall Hollow during the game. But they weren't the same. Everything was a lot more complicated than the stories let on.

Did the Committee know? Bailee wondered. No, she decided, Madison would have warned her. Even if things were weird between them right now, Madison never would have let Bailee or anyone play the game if she knew the truth. Madison would never put anyone in danger on purpose. Which meant . . . no one outside of the woods knew what was *really* going on.

Bailee slipped her phone from her pocket and pressed the home button again and again, willing it to blaze to life. But it sat dead in her hand, useless.

"Don't bother," said Abigail from up ahead, eyeing Bailee's phone. "Those things never work. Not during the game."

Bailee tucked the device away, fear squeezing her throat. With no phones and no outside help, they were on their own. With only a ghost to guide them.

"Maybe we should just . . . leave?" suggested Carmen. "That thing—the Specter—seems dangerous. Perhaps we should go tell—"

"No, you can't!" Fear sparked in Abigail's eyes. "If you all leave now, the game will be forfeited, and the Specter will win. One of you *needs* to ring the bell."

"Why?" asked Noah.

But Bailee didn't need to wait for Abigail's explanation; she already knew. She flipped through her Bellwoods journal, landing on an old entry. She read it out loud.

ENTRY #23

IF THE BELL ISN'T RUNG, TROUBLE WILL FOLLOW.

"Trouble?" asked Carmen, voice small.

Bailee nodded. She thought back to her conversation with Nan earlier. "My nan said the year after Abigail went missing, a lot of bad stuff happened. Crops died, businesses closed, people fought. . . ." Bailee turned to Abigail. "This is why, isn't it? It's the game. No one rang the bell that year, did they? And if no one rings the bell, the Specter is free to terrorize the town."

Abigail nodded. "One of you needs to ring the bell to end the game and keep the town safe. It only takes one."

"Can I ring the bell?" asked Noah. "I'm not actually playing. I'm just doing research."

"My friend—I mean, Fen—he's the other player," Bailee started. "But he ran off a little while ago."

Abigail frowned. "He shouldn't have done that." She started walking faster, beckoning for the others to keep up. "It's safer to stick together. The Specter prefers to hunt one-on-one. More fun that way, I guess. And easier, too. Players are more vulnerable when they're alone. If your friend is out there by himself . . ."

"Do you think the Specter's found him?" Bailee asked.

"Probably," said Abigail.

Bailee, Noah, and Carmen exchanged worried glances. No one spoke.

A far-off look came to Abigail's eyes. She shook it away. "We need to keep moving," she said. "It will be back soon."

CHAPTER 13
ENTER THE KEEPER

Carmen switched on her flashlight. The beam bounced along in front of them, creating monstrous shadows that flickered and danced. Above, branches scratched at the deepening sky like gnarled fingers. No one spoke. They listened, jumping at every snapping twig or crunching leaf.

"There's a path up ahead that will lead us to the river," said Abigail in a low voice. "From now on, stick together. The Specter will do everything it can to separate you."

"Is that what it did to me earlier? When I lost the path," said Carmen.

Abigail nodded. "The forest does the Specter's bidding during the game; you can't trust it. The paths are generally reliable, when you can find them. Fewer places for the Specter to hide."

Stick to the paths. Bailee thought back to what Arlo had said earlier—what they had *tried* to say. But Arlo had practically choked on the words. As if something had been keeping them from speaking.

"This is nuts. You're saying we can't even trust the ground we're walking on?" Noah asked, looking at the forest around him in disbelief.

"Not during the game," replied Abigail. "Once we get to the river, we'll follow it north toward the old bridge near Silver Falls. We'll climb up the embankment there. That's the fastest way to the bell."

They came to a vast patch of thorny bushes. Abigail stopped, face growing soft and puzzled. "Wait, what are we doing again?" She turned to Bailee, Carmen, and Noah. As if she'd suddenly forgotten all about them.

"We're going to the bell," prompted Carmen uncertainly.

"Oh. Right." Abigail gave a frustrated shake of her head. The hazy look in her eyes cleared. She scowled at the thorny patch in front of them. "We don't have time for this." She ran a pale finger down a thorny branch, and, as if alive, the bushes drew back. A path now ran through the center.

"Whoa!" cried Noah. "How did you do that?"

"Let's just say, the Specter isn't the only one with certain powers during the game," Abigail answered, breathing heavily, as if the trick had left her winded. "But mine won't last long. The Specter is stronger. Much stronger."

Minutes later they found themselves back on the path. They picked up the pace. Noah and Carmen jogged ahead, the beam of Carmen's flashlight guiding their way.

Bailee fell into step beside Abigail. "We're not the first group of kids you've led through the woods, are we?"

"Hmm?" said Abigail, as if Bailee's question had pulled her out of deep thought. "Oh yes. There have been others. I don't remember them all now. It's hard to keep the years straight. . . ." Abigail shook her head, a pained expression on her face. Her fingers went to her temples as if searching for the memories. "But they didn't always need me, the kids who come to play the game. Sometimes they saw me watching them and ran off, afraid. But I never meant to scare them; I just wanted to see. It gets lonely, here in the woods."

Bailee nodded. She knew how it felt to be lonely, especially these days. She couldn't imagine spending year after year wandering the woods, alone, with only the Specter-thing for company. And when people finally did take notice, they ran, scared. It sounded like a terrible existence.

"The kids used to win the game, easy. But one year they needed help," Abigail continued. "The Specter had grown too strong by then, too cunning. There was only one player left in the game. They were going to lose."

"So you stepped in and helped," said Bailee.

Abigail nodded, face grim. "The Specter was . . . not pleased by my intrusion. It's found ways to punish me over the years.

Unlike the kids who play the game, I don't have anything to give the Specter in exchange for safe passage out of the woods. So it has found other things to take." Abigail's hand went to her braid, fingers working the end of it.

"I don't understand," said Bailee. "Why haven't we heard about you helping during the game before? Why haven't we heard about the Specter?"

But Abigail didn't answer. Her eyes had taken on a soft, far-away look. Her mind had wandered again.

Bailee's hand went to her journal, tucked back in her waist-band. If the Specter caught her, at least she had something to give, something to get her home safe. It was a small consola-tion, but it was better than nothing.

Suddenly the sound of approaching footsteps made every-one freeze. Carmen and Noah whirled around. Someone was running up the path behind them, fast.

Carmen shone her flashlight in the direction of the approaching person.

"Be prepared to run," whispered Abigail, alert once more. She stood as still as a statue, but her eyes darted back and forth like a frightened rabbit sensing for danger.

The footsteps grew louder and louder.

Bailee tensed, and she watched Noah and Carmen do the same, bracing themselves for another attack. Then a figure walked out of the shadows.

"Hey! You're blinding me," said Madison. She shielded her eyes, warding off the flashlight's glare.

"Madison? What are you doing here?" Bailee ran and hugged her friend.

Carmen lowered her flashlight, and Noah sagged visibly with relief. Abigail shrank into the woods, blending in with the shadows.

"I can't believe I found you!" Madison squeezed Bailee, words spilling out in a rush like usual. But it wasn't exuberance that drove Madison now—it was panic. She trembled and shot fearful glances over her shoulder. "Everyone needs to get out of the woods. Now! It's not safe!"

"I know, Mads. There's—" Bailee started.

But Madison was too panicked to listen. "Look, I thought the game was all make-believe. Just a silly tradition, you know? But something felt off when I heard the bell earlier. The book of rules *said* the bell signaled the start of the game, but I didn't ring a bell. So who did?" She reached into the back pocket of her jeans and brought out the little book Jade had given her earlier. "But I thought, hey, no big deal, it's probably just Jade and Arlo—you know, the older grade playing a prank on us or something. Like, maybe that's all part of the game. But while we waited at the edge of the woods, things got really weird. We heard these noises—"

"Mads—" Bailee started again, but it was no use. Madison's panic was a runaway train. There was no stopping it.

"Then Arlo started getting really upset," she went on. "They were trying to say something to Jade about remembering—how kids never remember—but they couldn't get the words out. It was like they were choking or something. Arlo got all red in the face and flustered. But they managed to say a few more things. . . ."

Bailee nodded along. She was pretty sure she already knew what Arlo had been trying to communicate.

"Arlo said you all were in danger, that we never should have let you all go into the woods! I thought Arlo was just being dramatic at first, you know, maybe trying to play up the spookiness of the game or something. But we waited and waited, and you didn't come back. No one did. Then we heard more weird noises. I started to get really worried!"

"It's okay, Mads. But Arlo's right; there is something strange going on, but we can explain—" Bailee said.

"Wait, what are *you* doing here?" said Madison, looking past Bailee and squinting at Noah.

He waved, shooting Madison a smile that was more like a grimace. "When you didn't have a press pass for me, I decided to check out the game anyway. Don't worry," he said heavily, "I regret it now."

"Okay . . . ," said Madison with a confused shake of her head. "Wait, where's Fen?" She looked around, only now realizing they were a player short.

"He—" Bailee started.

But the sound of laughter cut her off. It came from the woods.

"Fen?" said Madison, whirling in the direction of the laugh. "Is that you?"

Bailee felt her fingertips tingle again. The laugh sounded like Fen's. But the timing was too convenient.

"Fen! Stop joking around. I'm calling the game. We need to leave." Madison charged up the path, following the sound of laughter.

"Mads, come back! We have to stay together!" Bailee ran after Madison, hand outstretched.

But it was too late. She watched in horror as Madison stepped off the narrow path, hand to her mouth, calling for Fen. In a matter of seconds, Madison was swallowed up by the woods.

CHAPTER 14
MYTHS AND MIST

They yelled for Madison. But it was no use. They heard her moving farther and farther away, calling for Fen.

Abigail emerged from the shadows. "Does she have something with her? A gift for the Specter?" she asked, words coming quick.

"Madison is on the Committee; she's not playing the game," said Bailee.

"Doesn't matter. The Specter will go after her anyway," replied Abigail, eyes searching the woods.

"But the rules—" Noah started.

"Anyone in the woods tonight is fair game for the Specter. There's nothing in the rules about that."

"That's not fair," said Carmen.

Abigail shrugged. "Rules are like that sometimes. A gift buys safe passage out of the woods. Once taken, you're safe from the Specter . . . more or less. But if you have nothing to sacrifice, well, the Specter will take something else. And it'll keep taking as long as it's given the chance."

"If she doesn't have a gift . . . ?" Bailee's heart quickened. She thought back to the story she'd shared with Noah earlier, the one about the boy losing his tongue. She had always thought the story was a joke. But now . . .

"I'm going to bring her back," Bailee said. "You all just stay here." And before anyone could argue, she bolted into the trees, yelling for Madison.

Bailee pushed against branches that clawed at her face. After a moment she spotted Madison up ahead, disappearing and reappearing between slanting tree trunks.

"Madison, stop! It's not safe!" Bailee called. But if Madison heard, she didn't listen. Bailee could hear her friend shouting for Fen, voice growing quieter and quieter as she moved deeper into the woods.

Soon she was gone.

Bailee ran a few more steps, then stopped. She put a hand to her eyes, straining to see. A strange mist had taken hold of the woods. It swirled in ribbons around the bases of trees and twined like mischievous cats around Bailee's ankles.

Her mind raced. Madison didn't know there was something more terrible than the ghost of Abigail Snook prowling the

143

woods. The Specter might find her any minute. It might find either of them.

"MADISON!" Bailee shouted. But it was no use. Her yell hit the wall of fog now pressing in around her and fell dead. All was quiet.

She took a breath. Madison was gone—there was nothing she could do about that now—and stumbling around in the forest alone, easy prey for the Specter, wasn't going to help. She needed to retrace her steps and get back to the path where the others were.

She backtracked. Fog swirled around her feet as she picked her way over the uneven terrain, tripping over rocks and roots. Overhead, branches raked the deepening sky. There was still time before night fell, but if she didn't get back to the others soon, she'd be wandering around in the woods in the dark, unable to see. Alone.

Just a few more steps, Bailee told herself. She hadn't gone that far into the woods, had she? The path and her friends were just ahead. They had to be.

After several minutes Bailee found herself in a small clearing. Fog clung to the edges, an impenetrable wall of gray mist. She called for her friends, then listened.

Only silence greeted her.

She pressed on, ignoring the fear rising inside her. She was just disoriented, that was all. But the longer she walked, the less she believed this was true.

Bailee stumbled into another clearing, one she recognized.

She felt a brief flicker of hope. But realization snuffed it out—this was the same clearing she'd passed a few minutes ago. She was going in circles. She was lost.

"Great," Bailee muttered, her words flattened by the fog.

Her friends had to be looking for her by now. Unless they had given up and moved on, trying to get to the bell before dark. Or, she thought with a stab of fear, the Specter had found them while waiting for her to return. If they had been caught, it would be all her fault. Gabby's insult echoed in her mind again—*she ruins everything*. Bailee was starting to feel like Gabby was right.

The sound of leaves crunching underfoot made her jump.

"Hello?" Bailee spun. Her fog-chilled fingertips went numb with fear. She braced herself, ready to run.

"Bailee?" came a familiar voice.

It was Abigail.

"Holy smokes," said Bailee, hand over her racing heart. "I never thought I'd be glad to hear Abigail Snook's voice in the woods."

Abigail laughed. Bailee heard the girl come closer, pushing through the trees.

"Where are the others?" Bailee called.

"Noah and Carmen are back this way. Madison and Fen are with them too."

Bailee exhaled with relief. "Can you lead the way? It's so hard to see."

"Of course. They're back behind me." Abigail appeared before Bailee now, just a silhouette against the swirling fog. Her voice sounded odd—flat and detached. But perhaps that was just the muffling effect of the woods and the mist.

"After you," Bailee said. She started walking toward the other girl.

But Abigail didn't move. A thin arm stretched through the fog toward Bailee.

"Grab my hand. We don't want you getting lost again," Abigail said.

Bailee started to reach for the girl. Then stopped. Fear pinged inside of her like a quiet but urgent alarm.

"Uh . . . why don't you just lead the way, and I'll stick close? Promise." Bailee had stopped moving. Her feet felt rooted to the forest floor. Her eyes were wide, focused on the silhouette that was Abigail—that was supposed to be Abigail—shifting gently against the curtain of fog.

"Come on," insisted the other girl. "We don't have much time. The Specter could be back any minute." The hand reached more urgently toward Bailee.

"No—no thanks," Bailee managed. She inched away, moving as silently as she could. The fog pressed in closer, bringing the shape of Abigail closer too.

"Bailee, I'm losing my patience," came her voice. A low growl now.

Bailee shivered. Her fear was a full-on scream of panic. How had she ever mistaken that voice for Abigail's? What she heard now was hard and cold and belonged to something much older and fouler than she had ever known. It was a voice that conjured images of mold and decay. One that made Bailee shiver.

She watched in horror as the shape of the thing that was not quite Abigail came closer. There were no footsteps this time, no snapping of branches or crunching of leaves. It glided, as silent as the fog. The pale arm stretched for her.

Bailee shrank away, feet slipping and sliding over the slick leaves carpeting the forest floor. Her hand went to her waistband. She plucked out her journal, holding it in front of her like a shield.

"Stay—stay away," she said in a strangled voice.

The silhouette of Abigail shrieked with glee. It came closer and closer.

Then the back of Bailee's legs connected with a fallen log. She toppled over it, arms flailing. She landed on her back with a hard thud that sent breath rushing from her lungs. Her journal went flying.

"Ouch," said the voice. "That's the thing about these woods, full of surprises. But don't feel bad. You're not the first to take a tumble."

The Specter stepped through the veil of fog, looking like Abigail's nightmarish twin. It still wore a cloak, but instead of a vibrant red, it was grayish green, hanging ragged from the Specter's spindly frame. The hood was pulled up, shrouding its face in shadow. Two green pinpricks of light blazed from within like glittering eyes. Hands the color of bone poked out from shredded sleeves with long fidgeting fingers.

Bailee scrambled backward, trying to put as much distance between herself and the Specter as possible. Her feet kicked up clumps of wet leaves and earth. Her hands groped wildly behind her, searching for her journal—her gift and only protection from the Specter.

"I remember a boy who took a tumble during the game, just like you did now," said the Specter, sounding almost wistful. "This was years ago, of course. I wonder sometimes if he ever misses this."

With horror, Bailee watched as the Specter pulled back the hem of its cloak and reached inside. She glimpsed a horde of treasures stashed within, jumbles of odds and ends. There were playing cards, tarnished rings, a compact mirror, and more. The Specter's pale hand rifled through the collection. Finally it fished out a glass marble.

A small moan escaped Bailee's lips as realization sank in—this marble had been someone's gift. Just like everything else within the Specter's cloak.

"The silly boy thought wolves roamed the woods. Can you imagine? His brother told him so, just to give the boy a fright. The boy had many nightmares after that. Until I took this off his hands." The marble gleamed between the Specter's fingers as if lit from within by a warm yellow flame.

Bailee said nothing. She didn't dare look away. She kept inching backward, fingers searching for her journal.

"I'm sure if he were here now, he'd thank me for taking this from him. His story is more useful to me anyway." The light within the marble began to pulse. "It's a good one, really. One of my favorites. I don't use it often—can be a bit tiring, you know? I save this one for special occasions. But I'll share it with you now, if you want. I can tell you appreciate a good scare."

Bailee shook her head in disbelief. The Specter sounded eager, almost like a child, asking if Bailee would like a bedtime story.

The Specter didn't wait for her answer. It held the marble up for Bailee to see, pinched carefully between two pale, mottled fingers. The small flame within began to flicker and grow bright. It turned a sickly shade of green, matching the Specter's eyes.

A howl followed, one like Bailee had never heard before.

The sound came from everywhere, rising, holding its pitch for so long that Bailee thought it might go on forever. She clapped her hands over her ears and snapped her eyes shut. Finally the howl died away, leaving a dreadful silence behind.

Bailee cracked one eye open and gasped.

Staring at her now was a monstrous wolf. It was bigger than any real wolf could be, by three times, at least. Green eyes blazed from behind a tangle of matted gray fur. Saliva dripped from enormous jaws. The wolf-monster licked its lips, revealing rows of long, jagged teeth.

Bailee had seen wolves in real life before, at a wildlife sanctuary she'd visited with her parents. She wasn't afraid of wolves, though she knew they should never be approached in the wild. But what loomed over her now was nothing like the wolves she saw that day. This was like something out of a nightmare.

Bailee yelped and scrambled backward.

"See?" the Specter spoke with a growl. "Powerful, isn't it? Now it's your turn to tell me a story—I can see you have a real knack for it. What will it be? Zombies in the graveyard?" The Specter-wolf dissolved before Bailee's eyes. Suddenly, a moldering corpse was standing before her. Brutal stitches stretched across its neck and face, and pieces of flesh dropped from it as it staggered toward Bailee, moaning.

She shrank away. She thought back to her conversation with Nan earlier, about outrunning zombies on her way home from school. But that hadn't actually happened; it was just a story.

"Maybe a different one?" The Specter dissolved into smoke again. It transformed into a pale woman in a dirty white gown with long, matted hair. The woman's eyes were hollow pits, lit from within by the glow of the Specter's green eyes. "What did you call her again? The Wailing Widow?" The Specter leered at Bailee.

My creative writing assignment, Bailee thought. *These are my stories. But how does it know?*

The Specter shifted shape again, back to its wolf form. It grinned at Bailee, baring its enormous teeth.

Bailee shuddered. Her hands searched for her journal in the underbrush. Without it, who knew what the Specter would take from her? She didn't want to find out.

Finally her fingertips brushed over something smooth and rectangular. Her journal.

The Specter's eyes glinted. "Come on. It's your turn now. Tell me your story, Bailee."

It charged at her, eyes blazing. Saliva flew from its snapping jaws. Bailee cried out, shrinking back in fear. She clutched her journal and squeezed her eyes shut.

Then the clearing was lit by a blinding light.

CHAPTER 15
GIFTS

The Specter howled in pain.

Bailee squeezed one eye open in time to see Carmen charge into view. She wielded her flashlight before her, the beam of light cutting through the fog and gloom like a blade.

"Hey! Beat it!" Carmen cried.

The Specter-wolf whimpered, then howled with fury, shrinking from the beam. It began to shrivel and stretch, twisting and twining like smoke caught in a breeze. It streamed away, disappearing into the trees.

The fog faded, and all around them the forest came into sharper focus.

"Is she okay?" Abigail asked—the real one this time—stumbling into the clearing.

It was Bailee's turn to be blinded. She raised an arm to shield her face, squinting against the flashlight's glare.

"Sorry," said Carmen, lowering the beam.

"Thought we lost you there for a moment," said Noah. He hurried over to Bailee and helped her up.

She wobbled as fear drained from her trembling legs. "Psh, can't get rid of me that easily."

"Did it . . . ?" Abigail started, pulling at her braid nervously.

Bailee flapped her journal at Abigail. She still had her gift. She was still in the game.

"'Beat it'?" Noah said, turning to Carmen with a laugh. "That's what you say when charging at a supernatural wolf-monster?"

Carmen shrugged. "It's, um, what we shout at raccoons when they get into our garbage bins at home. Is that weird?"

"No, it was awesome," said Noah.

"It got the job done," said Bailee, steadier now. "Thanks, Carmen."

Carmen smiled.

"Did you find Madison? Or Fen?" Bailee asked, absently brushing leaves and mud from her jeans.

The others shook their heads.

"We stayed on the path, calling. We didn't want to risk getting separated. But when we heard that howl, we came running," said Noah.

"You got here just in time. I thought I was wolf food." Bailee swiped at a scratch on her forehead with the sleeve of her jacket in frustration. Now that her fear had passed, she felt anger creeping in.

"We did too," said Noah grimly.

"Let's get going. We don't have much time," Abigail said. She started to turn and walk off into the woods.

"No," said Bailee, anger flaring. "No more running around in the woods, waiting for another surprise. I want to know what the game's really about."

Abigail's fingers fidgeted with the end of her braid again. But she said nothing.

"I saw the Specter's collection. All those gifts under its cloak? It's not just our gifts it wants. There's more to it, isn't there?" Bailee insisted.

Abigail nodded slowly. "It's not about the objects. It's what they . . . represent."

"That wolf I saw back there . . . ?"

"Stolen from some kid, long ago." Abigail sighed.

"But why? What does it do with them?" asked Carmen, clutching her flashlight.

Abigail chewed her lip, then continued in a whisper. "It *wears* them. Just like it wears my cloak. It uses stories as disguises.

But the more it takes, the more it needs. It's never satisfied. It's always hungry for more. . . ."

Abigail got a faraway look in her eyes again.

Bailee shook her head in disbelief. Fear and anger tangled inside her, forming a tight knot in her stomach. She pulled out her journal, jabbing a finger at the pages. "I don't understand. I've spent years collecting stories about the Bellwoods. Why isn't there any mention of the Specter? Why haven't I heard about any of this before?"

"Getting caught by the Specter—it's like a jolt to the mind," said Abigail, words coming more slowly now. "Your brain goes all blank, and you don't remember what happened. All you're left with is this sense that something is . . . missing. Feels like trying to remember a dream after waking. The more you try to hold the thoughts in your mind, the quicker they drain away."

"So kids who are caught during the game don't remember what's happened to them?" said Noah, pen and notepad in his hands again.

Abigail nodded again. "It's not just the kids who don't remember. I—I . . ."

"Abigail?" Carmen said, looking at her with concern.

But Abigail didn't answer. Her face had taken on a hazy look again, eyes wide and full of fear. Bailee could think of only one word to describe Abigail when she got like this—"lost."

Bailee shot a helpless look at Noah and Carmen. They wouldn't get any more answers for a little while. "C'mon, let's get going," Bailee said.

They walked out of the clearing and navigated back to the

path. Abigail moved along with them in a daze. Her eyes had a fearful, far-off look, one that was becoming more and more familiar.

Bailee studied their ghostly companion while they walked, mind whirring. Were Abigail's mental slips a side effect of being caught by the Specter too many times? She was struck by a sudden pang of sadness. Even in death, Abigail didn't have peace. Year after year her spirit returned to the woods, only to spend the night dodging the Specter's attacks, all to protect the kids who were playing and who would forget her once the game was done. It wasn't fair. There had to be a way to help Abigail. To stop the Specter, not just for one more year, but for good. Was that even possible?

Bailee's thoughts were interrupted by Carmen and Noah going as still as statues on the path in front of her. Bailee grabbed Abigail by her cloak to keep her from absentmindedly smacking into Carmen.

"Who's there?" said Noah, voice grim. "If you're the Specter, you'd better watch out. Carmen has her flashlight, and she's not afraid to use it. Right, Carmen?"

"Um—that's right," Carmen agreed. She flicked it toward the figure standing before them.

"Hey!" Fen squinted, blinking and rubbing his eyes.

"Sorry, necessary precaution." Carmen lowered the beam.

Abigail, alert again, shrank into the woods, out of sight.

"Where on earth have you been?" said Bailee, stomping

toward Fen, ready to pick up where their previous argument had left off. But as she got closer, she could see something was wrong. He was the sort of kid who laughed and rolled his eyes when he got in trouble. He accepted every dare, no matter how absurd or ill-advised, and he managed to break at least one bone in his body each year. None of that ever seemed to shake the arrogant smile from his face. But he wasn't smiling now. Fen was paler than usual. He swayed on his feet, looking like he might collapse at any moment. He looked small and help-less. Afraid.

Bailee's anger faded. She grabbed Fen's elbow and guided him to sit on a nearby stump.

"What happened?" asked Noah.

"I—I don't really know." Fen's forehead creased with con-centration. "One minute I was on my way to the cut, then—wait, where am I now?" He looked around as if noticing his surroundings for the first time. He opened his mouth to speak again, but he didn't get the chance.

Madison came running up the path toward them.

"Thank goodness!" she cried, not even flinching when Car-men turned her flashlight on her this time. "I've been looking everywhere for you all!"

Bailee rushed to her friend. The two girls nearly toppled over as Bailee wrapped her arms around Madison. And as relieved as Bailee was to see Mads safe and sound, she was even more relieved when Madison hugged her back just as tight.

"What are *you* doing here?" Fen asked.

Bailee could practically feel Madison roll her eyes before they pulled apart. "I've been looking for *you*, actually. Now that we're all together, we need to get out of here! There is something *super weird* happening. I don't think it's safe!"

"A little late with the breaking news, Mads. We already know." Fen grimaced, rubbing his temples as if trying to massage away a headache.

"Wait, you know about the Specter?" asked Carmen.

Fen raised an eyebrow at her. "I don't know what a Specter is, but I definitely ran into something weird out in the woods. And it wasn't trying to give me a nice hug." He moved to stand but staggered. Noah helped him sit back down.

"That's why we have to get out of here!" Madison stamped an impatient foot.

"You can't. Not until someone rings the bell," came Abigail's voice. She stepped forward out of the shadows.

Madison jumped. Beside her, Fen went even paler and scrambled to his feet, ready to run.

"Who—who?" Madison stammered, pointing at the ghostly girl.

"Everyone, chill," said Bailee. "We have a lot to fill you in on."

CHAPTER 16
TRUE STORIES

"**S**o she's the real Abigail Snook," said Madison.

Bailee nodded.

"But she's *not* hunting us?" asked Fen.

"Nope," said Abigail, shaking her head.

"But there *is* something hunting us?" Fen continued. Some color had returned to his face. He looked steady on his feet once more.

"Abigail calls it the Specter, a term that implies a haunting presence and disturbances of the mind. An apt name," said Carmen.

"Thank you," said Abigail, and Carmen nodded in return.

"The Specter looks like Abigail. But isn't," Noah chimed in.

"Hey, it doesn't look *exactly* like me," Abigail protested.

"So let me get this straight," Madison said, eyes wide with disbelief. "The game is real. But everything we thought we knew about Abigail is wrong. Despite that, we still need someone to ring the bell and end the game?"

"Yes," said Bailee, looking to Abigail, who nodded.

"And what if we just *don't* ring the bell?" Fen asked.

"Then the Specter will win the game and be unleashed from the woods, free to terrorize the whole town until next Halloween," said Abigail.

"Not ideal," said Noah.

"So we have no choice. We have to finish the game." Madison sat down on a rock and put her head in her hands.

"All the while the Specter will be picking us off one by one, stealing our gifts and feeding on our worst stories and memories," Bailee said with false cheer.

"Great. Solid options. Either way, everything sucks," grumbled Fen.

No one spoke for a moment.

"We have my flashlight," said Carmen. "The Specter can't stand the light. So far it's been effective at keeping the Specter at bay."

"Really?" said Madison, turning a hopeful face to Carmen. "That is a definite advantage." She got up and started pacing up and down the path as if having a problem to work out made digesting the fact that ghosts and apparitions were real more manageable.

"Look, there are five of us, and all we need is one person to make it to the bell. If we work together—" started Bailee.

But Madison was shaking her head. "Only official players can ring the bell. It's in the rules." She reached into the back pocket of her jeans and pulled out the small book Jade had given her earlier. She cracked it open and flipped through the pages. "See? Here, this part says Committee members . . . and game crashers"—she looked pointedly at Noah—"don't count. Only the chosen players can ring the bell and end the game."

"She's right," confirmed Abigail. "Official players only."

"Okay, so three of us, then," Bailee continued. "If we stick together and use Carmen's flashlight to fend off attacks until one of us three—"

"Two," Fen corrected her.

Everyone looked at him.

"I'm out," he said. "The Specter—or whatever—got me."

No one spoke for a moment. "How? When?" said Bailee finally.

"Earlier. After we . . . split up." Fen shoved his hands in his pockets and stared hard at the ground.

"You got caught? What was it like?" asked Noah, eyes wide with curiosity now. He brought out his pen and notepad again.

Fen thought for a moment, as if struggling to remember. His face turned grim. "There was a voice," he started. "I remember it was calling me from somewhere off in the woods. It sounded . . . strange, but kind of familiar, too. I thought it was Brendan or Luca. Maybe one of the older kids even, just someone playing a prank. So I followed, ready for a laugh. The voice was moving farther and farther away, deeper into the woods."

"Sounds a little like what happened to me earlier, by the cave," Carmen murmured.

"I followed the voice for a while, but then it stopped. Like whoever it was just disappeared. Suddenly I could feel someone behind me, breathing down my neck."

"Who was it?" whispered Madison.

"This is the unbelievable part . . . because"—Fen shook his head—"you were right, Bailee. I made it all up. That story I told you earlier—none of it was real. But, somehow, there he was, standing right behind me—Ben Bradley."

Bailee didn't say anything, just nodded. This sounded exactly like what had almost happened to her in the fog earlier when the Specter had turned into a zombie and her Wailing

Widow. Somehow the Specter knew their stories and used those stories against them.

"I knew he couldn't be real, but at the same time . . . I knew it was him," Fen continued. "He looked even more horrible than I'd imagined—all green and moss-covered, like he'd been lying around in the woods for years. There was some sort of fungus growing on his skin, and his eyes were nothing but blank, empty spaces lit by a weird green light. He was smiling at me. His teeth were all rotting and black." Fen shuddered. "But the worst was when he whispered."

..Fen..

Fen...

..Fen..

Bailee and her friends exchanged uneasy looks.

"He just stood there, grinning and whispering at me. I stumbled away, but he crept closer and closer, reaching out with his disgusting hand and smiling that awful, rotting grin. Then it was like my mind went blank. I—I don't remember anything else." Fen had gone pale again, as if he were about to be sick. He leaned against the trunk of a tree for support. "The next thing I knew, I was back on the path, a flashlight in my eyes, surrounded by you all."

"And your gift?" asked Abigail.

Fen stuck a hand in his jeans pocket, searching for his game die. "Gone. I don't even remember the thing taking it."

"They never remember . . . ," murmured Madison, almost to herself. "That's what Arlo said to me before I came into the woods. It didn't make sense before, but now—this is what they must have meant. Players don't remember being caught or anything that happened in the woods while playing the game."

"But if Arlo tried to warn you, they must remember something," said Noah.

Madison didn't say anything. She paced back and forth again, a thoughtful look on her face.

"Great. Arlo and Jade knew all this was going to happen? They couldn't have told us *before* we came into the woods?" Fen said.

"I don't think Jade knows," said Madison. "She would have told me."

"Arlo *tried* to tell us, remember? But it was almost like the words wouldn't come. They kept choking and spluttering. It was like some—*force*—was preventing them from speaking," said Noah.

"So no one can remember what happens during the game except the winner. But they can't talk about it," said Bailee. "But why? Why erase people's memories, and why keep them from talking?"

They turned to Abigail expectantly. She shrugged. "I still don't fully understand how the game works. But would you all have signed up to play if you knew the truth?"

Bailee and her friends looked at one another. Would they?

"All I know is the game keeps happening, year after year," Abigail continued. "The only part that changes are the kids who play. And the Specter, of course. It's been growing more and more powerful with each game. And the rest . . . the rest . . ." A pained expression creased Abigail's face. "I'm sorry, I can't remember. I have so much trouble remembering. . . ." She looked lost again.

"It's okay. You've been a huge help so far," said Bailee, putting a reassuring hand on the girl's shoulder.

Everyone was silent. Their eyes kept straying to the shadow-choked woods.

"Look," said Bailee finally. "Carmen and I are still in the game. And Carmen's a force to be reckoned with, thanks to her flashlight." She paused, shooting a reassuring smile at

Carmen. "We've got to at least try to get to the bell and end this thing."

Everyone nodded.

"Lead the way, then," said Fen. He dusted off his hands.

"Wait. You're coming with us?" said Madison, incredulous. "But the Specter took your gift. You have free passage out of the woods. Don't you want to go home?"

Fen stared at her as if this were the most ridiculous statement he had ever heard. "Of course I'm coming with you. First of all, you dorks need all the help you can get. Second, this is the most exciting thing that's happened in Fall Hollow since, like, *ever*, and I'm not going to miss it. Third . . ." Fen paused. "Now that I've seen the Specter in action, I wouldn't wish one of its attacks on my worst enemies."

Fen's gaze landed pointedly on Bailee. She felt her cheeks grow warm and her jaw clench. Even while being hunted by some story-stealing spirit, Fen had to bring up their fight.

"Really, Fen? You don't think we have bigger things to worry about right now?" She pushed past him and marched down the path.

"I just want to know why," he grumbled, following. "Why did you rat me out to Bright about the dare? We're supposed to be friends, Bailee—"

"I already told you, it wasn't me! It's not my fault you don't believe me," Bailee snapped back.

"But if it wasn't you, then who? Who else could it have been?

Everyone else got in trouble. Everyone except you," Fen argued.

"And me!" added Carmen, but they ignored her.

Bailee whirled around to face Fen. She opened her mouth to shout at him, but someone else spoke instead.

"Stop arguing. *Just stop!*" Madison shouted.

Everyone turned.

Madison looked small against the towering gloom of the woods. She stared at her feet, a pained expression on her face. Her shoulders fell as she let out a big sigh. She looked like someone coming to a very difficult decision. "It was me, okay." Her voice was a choked whisper. "I'm the one who told Bright about the dare."

No one spoke. Overhead, leaves whispered and branches creaked.

"I knew the dare was a bad idea," Madison continued. "I even tried to talk you out of it, Fen, remember? But you wouldn't listen."

Fen stared at Madison, mouth open.

"You could have hurt yourself. You're always doing dangerous stuff, but lately it's almost like you're *trying* to hurt yourself. I knew that if you went ahead with the dare, you were putting yourself in real danger this time . . . so I told Principal Bright." Madison's eyes were brimming with tears now. "I didn't know what else to do."

For once Fen was speechless; he had no quips or sarcastic comebacks.

Bailee felt equally tongue-tied. Realization dawned on her, a feeling like when she finally got a math problem right after the fifth try—this was why Madison had been so distant with her lately. She hadn't been drifting away from Bailee or mad about getting detention like the rest of their class. Madison had felt guilty.

"I'm sorry, Fen. I'm sorry for getting you and everyone else in trouble. And Bailee . . ." Madison turned to her friend, eyes glassy with tears now. "I didn't want people to know it was me who told, so I showed up for the dare and took a detention along with everyone else. But then . . ." She threw her arms up helplessly. "You weren't at the falls and gone from school for the rest of the day. Gabby told everyone she saw you talking to Principal Bright before we got busted at the falls. Everyone started blaming you. I'm so sorry, Bailee. I didn't mean for that to happen."

No one spoke for a long time. Everyone looked nervously from Madison to Bailee.

"How . . . How could you not have told me?" Bailee finally spluttered, not knowing what else to say.

"I didn't want you to be mad at me! I—I didn't want anyone to be mad at me," said Madison, eyes fixed on the ground.

"So you just let everyone be mad at *me* instead?" Bailee said, voice rising.

Tears welled in Madison's eyes. "I'm so, *so* sorry, Bailee. I tried to defend you. I really did! But no one would listen; no one believed me. The way it looked . . . They'd made up their minds already. I'm *so* sorry."

Bailee's jaw clenched. All her anger about the unfairness from the past few weeks was roaring inside of her—the gossip and nasty comments at school, her mom and dad never being home, her worries about Nan being snatched away by a stroke. Now this? All the things she wanted to say, *needed* to say, were bursting to get out all at once.

But when she tried to speak, the words wouldn't come.

So she said nothing.

Bailee took a deep breath. Her anger burned hot inside of her like a sparkler, those little hand-held fireworks Nan used to buy her for summertime campfires. Bailee imagined her anger as one of those sparklers now, blazing bright and hot. She let the feeling burn itself out and go cold.

She breathed again. Her jaw relaxed. Her anger quieted. But it didn't go away.

"Bailee . . . ," Madison started.

But Bailee shook her head. "We don't have time for this." Her voice was flat and firm.

She turned and marched down the path. The sound of footsteps told her that the others were following.

Everyone walked in silence, no one knowing quite what to say. They marched through the woods, rounding one bend, then another. Minutes passed. Finally, one by one, they staggered to a stop.

Before them a steep cliff rose sharply toward the sky. Moss hung from the rocky ledges, and small trees jutted out from crevices at strange angles. The path wound toward it, then slithered into a narrow gap in the cliff face, disappearing into darkness.

They had made it to the cut.

CHAPTER 17
THE CUT

"**P**lease don't tell me we're going in there," said Noah with a groan.

Bailee took a tentative step toward the cut and peered inside. During the day it was just a narrow passage through the cliff. But now, with night closing in, it felt like a monstrous, gaping mouth, ready to snap shut and swallow up trespassers at any moment.

Carmen crept toward the opening and shone her flashlight inside. "Looks safe enough. Just a bunch of dirt and cobwebs."

"Cobwebs?!" Noah groaned again. "There's no other way we can take?"

"Following the river is the quickest way to the bell," said

Bailee. "And the river is on the other side of these cliffs. We could walk around or try climbing up and over, but that would take forever."

"It's the quickest way," Abigail agreed.

Was it Bailee's imagination, or did their ghostly companion look different? Stretched or thinner somehow. Her face was paler, and dark semicircles, like bruises, now rimmed the bottom of her eyes. She'd been growing quieter and quieter, speaking only when needed. Bailee had noticed her staring off into the distance more frequently as if lost in thought.

"Last time I got too close to a hole in a cliff, bats flew at my head," said Noah, edging away from the opening.

"How do we know the Specter isn't already in there waiting for us?" said Madison, peering nervously into the dark passage.

Then a voice came to them. One like branches rattling in an autumn wind. "Because I'm out here, watching you."

They all jumped.

"Go!" Abigail shouted.

Carmen dove into the narrow crevice. The beam of her flashlight threw the passage into sharp relief. Shadows flickered and danced, running from the light.

Bailee and Madison followed with Abigail close behind. Noah scrambled after them with Fen bringing up the rear.

"Move, go faster!" Fen yelled, looking behind him, eyes wide with panic.

But it was slow going through the narrow crevice. Tangles

of roots caught at their clothes and hair. Their feet slipped on slick rocks and wet leaves. Dirt rained down on them from above, accompanied by an unsettling skittering sound.

"This is . . . unpleasant," said Carmen, spluttering as she barreled through a wall of cobwebs.

"Just keep moving," said Abigail.

"You can't run forever," came the Specter's leering voice, echoing along the passage after them.

"Can we pick up the pace?" Fen shouted. "I'd like to *not* get caught by that thing again."

"Going as fast as I can," called Carmen. "Do you need my flashlight?"

"No, no!" Fen answered too quickly. "Just go. Don't look back here."

Noah groaned. "You know saying something like that invites questions. . . ."

"Trust me," said Fen in a voice edged with fear. "Don't look back."

Bailee felt goose bumps prick up her arms at Fen's words. Fresh fear fluttered in her stomach. More scuttling sounds came from overhead.

"Hurry!" Bailee yelled.

"Come on, friends. It's just a game. Aren't you having fun?" came the Specter's taunting voice, echoing all around them.

The cut narrowed the deeper they went. They pressed on, twisting and sidestepping through the rocky crevice. They were about halfway through when a rumble shook the ground beneath them.

"Uh, what is that?" Noah yelled over the noise.

It was a sound like thunder. Stones rained down from above, and the rocky walls of the cut trembled. Then they began to move.

"What is happening?" Fen shouted.

"It's trying to crush us!" Madison screamed, watching in horror as the gap in the cliffs started to squeeze shut on either side of them.

The Specter let out another shriek of glee.

"I don't think so," Abigail muttered. She extended her arms out on either side, pushing against the rocky walls. She shut her eyes, concentrating. The advancing walls of the cut began to slow.

"Yes! It's working!" Bailee yelled.

Beads of sweat dotted Abigail's forehead as she continued to push. The rock walls trembled again, then finally shuddered to a stop.

"Whoa! How—" Madison started. But there was no time to marvel at Abigail's powers. Bailee was already yanking Madison by the hand, scrambling for the exit.

"Abigail! Are you okay?" Noah put a hand on the girl's back as she wobbled, unsteady on her feet. She slumped forward, exhausted.

"Seriously, folks, *we have to move!*" came Fen from behind them.

"Help me get her through," said Noah. He and Fen worked together, guiding Abigail through the last stretch of the passage. Behind them, the skittering sound grew louder and louder.

"Almost there!" cried Carmen. With one last burst she pushed out of the cut. Bailee and Madison stumbled out behind. The ground outside sloped down steeply toward the Hollow River, and they almost went sprawling.

"Any sign of the Specter?" asked Madison, recovering her footing. She scanned the trees crowded close to the river's edge.

Carmen moved her flashlight over the terrain. "Looks clear," she said, then turned, flicking the beam back into the mouth of the cut where Noah and Fen struggled with a dazed Abigail.

What she saw almost made her drop her flashlight.

"What? What is it?" said Bailee, dread surging. Against her better judgment, she peered into the cut.

Spiders. Too many spiders. More spiders than should ever be allowed in one place. The walls of the narrow crevice rippled with thousands of scuttling bodies. The spiders flooded through the passage, creeping toward Noah, Fen, and Abigail like a slow-motion wave about to crash over them.

It was a horrifying sight, and Bailee wasn't even afraid of spiders. Not like . . .

Noah and Fen emerged from the cut, dragging Abigail along with them. She collapsed to her hands and knees. Noah helped her lean against the side of the cliff. Fen, who knew what was crawling through the cut behind him, scrambled to put as much distance between him and the advancing spider horde as possible.

"What's wrong?" asked Noah, noting Fen's panic-stricken face. Noah peered into the cut.

"Don't—" Bailee started.

But Noah had already seen the spiders. He screamed. Bailee didn't blame him. The sight was the stuff of nightmares.

"What is—HOLY!" yelled Madison, turning at the sound of Noah's cry. She jumped back.

Spiders poured from the opening of the passage. Thousands of them. They crawled over one another, dropping to

the ground, leaping, flinging themselves from the cliff. They marched forward, a strange, scuttling army, all moving in the same direction—toward Noah.

He backed away. His mouth was frozen open in shock. He tripped over a rock and fell back into a large tree. He flattened himself against the trunk, trying to make himself as small as possible. The spiders flowed toward him.

"Why is this happening?" Carmen yelled.

"Noah's afraid of spiders," Bailee called back. "He mentioned it earlier. The Specter must know!"

Carmen swung her flashlight toward the squirming mess of tiny bodies streaming across the ground. They hissed and scurried away from the beam, but it didn't stop them. "This isn't working as well as I'd hoped," she cried, moving the flashlight around and around. The spiders evaded the beam, ebbing and flowing around it.

A laugh came from inside the cut, echoing toward them like the sound of a gathering storm.

"Watch for the Specter! The spiders are just a distraction!" yelled Abigail.

"Well, it's working!" Madison called back, looking help-lessly at the arachnids surging past her feet.

"Keep the flashlight on the cut! Don't let the Specter get close!" Bailee directed Carmen. Then she rushed over to Noah, standing between him and the spiders. She tried kicking dirt in their path. She tried blocking their way. But the river of march-ing bodies just flowed around her.

"Ugh!" Bailee stamped in frustration. She always took great pains to relocate spiders when they turned up in her house. But there wasn't a glass jar in the world big enough to contain all these.

Finally, face screwed up in a reluctant grimace, she began to stomp.

Madison and Carmen rushed over to join. Madison clasped a hand to her mouth, holding in a scream.

"Sorry! Sorry! Sorry!" said Carmen with every crushing blow. "Normally you are useful, *perfectly nice* creatures. But tonight you need to leave Noah alone!"

"Yeah, just chill, you jerks!" Fen joined the fray, spiders crunching as he jumped up and down.

The sound of squelching, flattening bodies made Bailee's stomach turn. She swallowed hard and redirected her attention to Noah. He was crouched, frozen, against the base of a tree. "Noah, don't run off, okay? Don't go off on your own—that's what the Specter wants," she said, keeping her voice as calm and even as she could.

"Yeah, Noah. They're just spiders," Madison said, trying to comfort him.

"It's likely Noah has arachnophobia, an irrational but intense fear of spiders," said Carmen between stomps. "Regardless of the actual danger presented, the triggering object or situation invokes excessive panic. He can't control his reaction."

"It's okay, Noah! We'll stop them!" shouted Fen.

But Noah wasn't listening. He fell back, scrambling away on all fours like a crab. He ignored the spiders marching toward him and instead gaped in horror at the mouth of the cut. His whole body began to tremble.

Bailee followed his gaze and yelped.

A spider, roughly the size of a horse, was wriggling itself out of the crevice. It was a stormy gray color, with long legs that

twitched and quivered. Eight liquid eyes blinked at her. Then with a sickening pop it pulled itself free from the cliff's crevice. It darted for Noah.

Fen shouted and Madison screamed.

Carmen swung her flashlight, trying to frame the enormous spider in its beam. But the monster just hissed and dodged.

"It's the Specter!" Abigail yelled.

"Noah, keep still!" said Carmen. She switched tactics and swung the beam of her flashlight toward him, trying to encircle him in its protective glow.

But Noah was too panicked. "Where did it go? I can't see it!" He pushed backward, farther into the woods.

"Noah!" Bailee shouted. "Watch—"

His foot connected with a log. He fell, crashing out of sight into the dense underbrush.

"No!" Carmen cried, running toward him. But something blew past her.

The Specter was on Noah in an instant.

CHAPTER 18
AT THE RIVER'S EDGE

By the time Carmen's flashlight found Noah, it was too late.

The Specter-spider laughed, a high-pitched scream of delight. Then it shrank and twisted away, dissolving into a gray cloud. It vanished into the trees like chimney smoke caught on the wind.

In a blink the mass of spiders vanished, as if they'd never been.

"Noah! Are you okay?" Bailee pushed her way through the tangle of bushes lining the riverbank, toward the boy.

He sat upright against a fallen tree. His eyes were wide and unseeing, face stretched in fear. He muttered like someone talking in their sleep.

The pen, usually clipped to his coat pocket, was gone.

"He'll be okay in a few minutes. Just needs to come out

of it," said Fen grimly, recognizing the aftermath of the Specter's attack. He waded into the bushes after Bailee. He reached down and tugged Noah to a standing position, then wrapped an arm around him, guiding him out of the trees. Bailee followed, steadying Noah from the other side.

"Come out of—what?" asked Madison, hovering nervously at the edge of the river. She'd missed most of Abigail's earlier explanations about the Specter.

"The Specter's touch does something to people's minds," said Abigail. She was on her feet again but paler than before, breathing heavily. "He'll be fine. He just won't remember much about what happened."

"Maybe that's for the best, if he won't remember the spiders," said Carmen.

Noah murmured agreeably.

They moved along the bank of the river. Tall cliffs soared up into the sky on either side. Logs and branches littered the water's edge and trees dotted the steep slopes, tilting at wild angles as they stretched to fill the gap created by the river. To Bailee's eyes, the trees looked as if they had tumbled from the cliffs and were now caught in a slow-motion slide, falling imperceptibly toward the river. And their deaths.

Above the doomed trees, the sky had taken on cotton candy hues. Normally Bailee would have found the sight beautiful. But tonight it made her heart race. The sun was setting, and night was on its way.

They had to hurry.

No one spoke as they trudged upriver. Madison kept shooting pleading looks at Bailee, but Bailee pretended not to notice. Madison's confession about the dare sat heavy in her stomach like a stone. Anger sparked in her anytime she thought too much about it. With a shake of her head, she put her friendship troubles out of her mind. They had bigger things to worry about right now.

Fen no longer needed to support Noah. The boy sleepwalked along beside them, his expression still glassy-eyed and dazed.

"Was this what I was like when you found me?" Fen asked, redirecting Noah as he made to stumble toward the river. "His expression is the same one I make during all of Owens's boring classes." Fen let his face go slack, eyes glazed.

"Owens isn't that bad," murmured Abigail.

Bailee stopped and turned to Abigail, tilting her head. "You know Mr. Owens?"

"Oh," said Abigail, looking uncertain at first. Then a small smile blossomed. "He was one of my teachers—I think? Yes . . . I remember now. Science. Sixth Grade. Wow, I haven't been able to remember anything from before the woods in—well, I don't know how long." For a moment Abigail's weariness subsided. She suddenly looked more solid, less like a ghost and more like the living person she used to be.

Bailee studied Abigail with a curious expression. The

ghostly girl had trouble remembering what had happened a few moments ago, but now Fen's passing mention of Mr. Owens had jarred a memory loose. *Maybe,* Bailee wondered, *with a little prodding, Abigail might remember more.* "Did he have that same poster, the one with the dissected frog, when you had him?"

Abigail's smile widened. "Ugh, yes. It was super gross. I hated looking at it every day. I can remember his classroom now, what he looked like. And his voice. Does he still tell those hilarious stories?"

"You must still be having trouble remembering if you think his stories are funny," said Fen with a wry grin.

Abigail laughed.

"What else do you remember?" murmured Noah sleepily.

Bailee snorted, looking over at the boy, now starting to stir. Even in a Specter-induced daze, Noah couldn't help but ask questions.

Abigail thought for a moment, and then her face fell. "I . . . I . . ." She shook her head in frustration. The lost look had returned; she fought to hold it off. But it was no use. Her mind slipped again.

Meanwhile Noah stretched as if waking from a long nap. Then he groaned, taking in his surroundings. "Uh . . . where am I?"

"Welcome back to the Bellwoods Game," said Fen ruefully.

Noah patted his breast pocket absently. His face fell. "My pen . . ."

"Sorry," said Bailee. "It's part of the Specter's collection now."

"Did it take my notepad, too?" Noah rummaged in his pockets, searching.

"It's here," said Carmen. She pulled it from her coat pocket. "I found it in the bushes after . . . you know."

Relief flooded Noah's face. He flipped through his notes, checking that they were all intact. "Thanks, Carmen." Then he slapped his forehead as if struck by a sudden realization. "Can someone please tell me that being chased by an enormous spider-monster was all just a terrible dream?"

"It was all just a dream," said Carmen helpfully. "But also, I'm lying. Sorry."

Noah groaned again.

"If it makes you feel any better, you won't remember most of this when the game's over," said Abigail with a sad smile.

"You know, normally that would be a bad thing. But in this case it might be okay." Noah rubbed his temples. "Ugh, let's get to the bell, finish this game, and get out of here."

"Noah, the Specter took your gift. You have safe passage out of the woods. You don't have to keep doing this. It's not safe," said Bailee, gesturing at the woods around them.

"Hey," he said. "I came into the woods looking for answers. And now that I know what's going on in the woods—what's *really* going on—I'm not leaving until all of us can."

Bailee smiled. "Okay."

They hurried along the bank in silence, listening for signs of the Specter's return. They came to a shallow stretch of river. Rocks dotted the fast-moving surface like stepping-stones, forming a sort of bridge all the way across.

"The bell is just up there," said Abigail, pointing at a rocky ridge rising from the opposite bank. "We'll cross here."

Carmen went first. Her flashlight beam bounced as she hopped from stone to stone. Abigail, Fen, and Noah followed with Bailee and Madison close behind. They wobbled as they jumped from one rock to another, heading for the opposite bank.

"Bailee?" Madison whispered as they went.

But Bailee didn't reply. She picked her way across the rocks, balancing with arms extended on either side.

"B-Bailee," Madison said again, louder this time.

"I don't feel like talking yet, okay, Mads?" Bailee leaped from the final rock and landed on the riverbank behind the others.

"It's not that. Look."

With a heavy sigh, Bailee stopped and turned around to face her friend.

Madison was perched on a wide, flat rock, only halfway across the river. She was staring intently at something in the river below her.

"Mads? What's wrong?" said Bailee, sudden fear squeezing at her throat.

"There's s-s-something down there." Madison pointed to the murky water.

"What's happening?" called Carmen from the bank. The beam of her flashlight glided over the river's surface.

"The Specter is up to something. I feel it," said Abigail. Her tired, wary eyes scanned the shadows pressing in close all around them.

"Come on, Mads. We have to go," Fen urged, stepping back out onto a rock toward Madison.

But Madison didn't answer. She stared into the water, fear stretching her face. "D-d-do you see? There's someone down there."

"The water can't be more than a couple feet deep here," said Noah, looking up and down the river. "How could someone be hiding under the water? It'd be impossible."

"The Specter can make anything possible," Abigail replied.

"Wait! Can you hear that?" Madison said. Her voice had gone taut like the string of a bow stretched back. "They're . . . coming."

"Who?" said Bailee. But she heard for herself soon enough.

The voices came from everywhere all at once. They sounded muffled and far away but grew louder and louder. They were chanting something. Bailee strained to hear.

"What are they saying?" said Fen, eyes darting all around.

"I can almost make it out." Carmen paused, listening. The voices grew louder as if in answer.

Fair is foul, and foul is fair. Fair is foul, and foul is fair. The voices chanted over and over again.

"What is that supposed to mean?" said Noah, perplexed.

"It's a quote. I recognize it from somewhere. . . ." Carmen's mind worked. Then finally, it clicked. "It's from the Scottish play."

"The—what?" asked Fen.

Bailee almost seconded his confusion, but Carmen's words rang familiar in her mind. Suddenly she knew where she'd heard them before.

The Tragedy of Macbeth.

Madison had practically begged Bailee to see it with her

when it was playing at the Gemstone, Fall Hollow's community theater, two years ago.

A four-hundred-year-old-play? Bailee had moaned. *Isn't it going to be, like, super boring?*

But Madison had insisted it wouldn't be. And she'd been right.

Bailee's doubts vanished as soon as the curtain rose. Sure, she found the dialogue hard to follow at times, but she couldn't look away. The play wasn't boring at all. It was about war and prophecies, ghosts and witches, revenge and murder. It was everything Bailee could have wanted in a play and more.

Madison didn't feel the same. She'd spent most of it hiding behind her hands, too queasy to watch. She didn't share Bailee's enthusiasm for all things spooky, and this play had leaned into the scares—hard. She'd been particularly frightened by the witches who'd opened the show. They appeared onstage, twisted and gnarled, looking ancient beyond the bounds of mortal life. They cackled and whirled around a strange fire, speaking to their animal familiars and foretelling the future of a Scottish general named Macbeth. Many acts of murder followed before Macbeth met his tragic fate.

Madison was visibly shaken after the show. Bailee guessed her friend hadn't been expecting so much horror and death in a stage play. While Madison's parents chatted with friends in the cast, they slipped out of the theater and into a little shop next door. It was a narrow space lined with dusty shelves. Old books and random odds and ends overflowed from the shelves. In a box full of tiny figurines shaped like cats and frogs, Bailee found a silver ring with stars etched into the band. She paid the storekeeper, a small man with a kind smile, using her allowance money. Then she presented the ring to Madison. Bailee told her the ring held a protection spell, one that would keep terrible witches away.

Madison had laughed but accepted the present. She knew there was no such thing as a protection spell or witches, at least not like the ones from the play. But Bailee thought she looked braver after putting on the ring. Madison had worn it every day since.

Bailee spied the ring now, glinting on her best friend's trembling hand, as Madison was still perched on the rock in the middle of the river. She looked frozen in place as she stared off into the water.

"Mads, it's the Specter; it has to be. We need to go now," said Bailee. She hurried to the river's edge and started to step out onto one of the rocks. But with a sudden scrape and a splash, the rock closest to her sank below the surface.

"How—" But the rest of her words were drowned out by more splashes.

One by one, all the stepping-stones they'd used to cross the river sank. Madison's was the only one that remained. Alone against the inky black stretch of water, her rock was like a circular stage with Madison frozen in the middle, an unwilling performer.

"Enough of this." Fen splashed into the river up to his knees, beckoning to Madison. "Forget using the rocks to cross! Let's go!"

But Madison shook her head, staring in terror at the water below. "I—I can't," she managed. "They'll get me."

"Who?" said Fen, shaking his head in frustration.

At that, the chanting grew louder and louder around them. There were new words now. Shakespeare's words. Ones that made fear tingle in Bailee's fingertips.

By the pricking of my thumbs, something wicked this way comes!

CHAPTER 19
THE THREE

The chanting rose to a fever pitch. The water around Madison began to bubble and boil. Then with a splash, a gnarled hand shot out of the water, reaching for Madison's ankle. She screamed and jumped away from it.

"Behind you!" shouted Noah.

Another hand sprang up on the other side of the rock. It was pale and splotched with green. It grabbed for Madison, but she scrambled away, forced to the center of her rocky perch. She spun in a circle, terror etched on her face. On either side, the horrible hands reached for her. She was trapped.

Carmen splashed into the shallows of the river, shivering as icy river water flooded her boots. She turned her flashlight on the nightmarish sight.

The hands flinched away from the beam. One after the other, they dropped below the surface of the water, out of sight.

"You got this, Carmen! Keep the Specter away!" said Bailee. Then she and Noah charged into the river after Fen, searching for any sign of the Specter. They didn't know what it had planned for Madison. But they had to do something, didn't they? They couldn't just leave Madison out there alone.

Fen splashed through the rushing water toward the rock where Madison sat, frozen in fear. He reached out for her. Then he slipped, nearly losing his footing. All around him the water began to rush and rise. It rose over his knees, inching higher and higher. The swift current tugged at his legs, threatening to sweep him off his feet and carry him away.

"Stay back!" Fen called to Bailee and Noah. "The Specter's making the water rise!"

"Here!" Abigail hurried to the river's edge. She plunged her pale hands into the icy water. She squeezed her eyes shut, concentrating. As if by magic, stillness rippled from her hands. The calm radiated out into the rushing river, turning the water as smooth as glass.

Then Abigail cried out in alarm.

She yanked her hands from the water. With them came ropes of thick, green goo—algae, the kind that choked stagnant waterways. They clung to Abigail's wrists, tightening around her like snares. Then they began to drag her forward, down into the river.

"Abigail!" Bailee yelled. She and Noah splashed back to the riverbank toward their ghostly friend. They grabbed at the green muck encircled around her wrists, pulling it away in clumps. But more and more ropes of algae leaped from the river. They latched onto Abigail's neck and braid, dragging her under.

"No!" Bailee screamed. She and Noah grabbed the girl's shoulders, trying to keep her head above the surface of the water. Abigail thrashed even as the green ropes pulled her farther and farther into the river's murky depths.

Carmen swung her flashlight, framing Abigail in the beam. The algae released, hissing and dissolving under the glare. Bailee and Noah dragged Abigail away from the water. She slumped against them, weak and spent.

Then they heard Madison scream.

A gnarled hand burst from the water and grabbed hold of Madison's rock. Another appeared beside it. A pale, sunken face emerged from the water next, with shoulders not far behind. A cloaked figure hoisted itself out of the river and climbed onto Madison's rock. Dripping tangles of hair hung from its skull-like head. Its milky white skin was splotched with green, like something dredged up from the river bottom. Its eyes were hollow sockets with the Specter's green, glittering eyes glowing within.

Bailee gasped. It was one of the witches from the play. Well, not exactly like the ones from the play. This one was even scarier. Because the corpselike face grinning at Madison now wasn't an actor wearing stage makeup; this was happening for real.

The Specter-witch reached for Madison. She screamed again and shrank away, scrambling to the farthest edge of her rocky perch.

Carmen swung her flashlight beam toward the Specter. But as she did, something burst from the water in front of her.

Another witch stood before Carmen. It was wrapped in rags that clung and dripped. It grinned at her with a mouth full of crumbling teeth and lurched forward.

"Watch out!" Fen yelled as the witch extended a hand toward Carmen.

She stumbled backward in alarm, arms pinwheeling. She dropped her flashlight. It splashed into the river and was immediately dragged downstream by the current. Carmen backed away from the witch until her feet found the riverbank. The witch sneered, then turned and waded through the rushing water toward Madison.

Fen splashed through the now waist-deep water, scrambling after Carmen's flashlight. It bobbed up and down with the waves, tossing light in wild directions. It smashed into rocks and logs as it was swept along by the current. After a few moments, the handle snagged on a hollow log. Fen ran for it.

On the rock, the first witch was advancing on Madison. All around her the river continued to churn and bubble.

Bailee and Noah watched on helplessly from the riverbank. "What do we do?" said Noah, kneeling over Abigail, who was lying unconscious on the ground.

Bailee scrambled to her feet and waded back into the river. The turbulent water pulled at her legs, threatening to drag her under, but she fought to stay upright. She searched the scene before her, a wary look in her eyes. Two witches had appeared, but in the play there'd been three. She was sure one more lay in wait, but where?

Madison trembled as the Specter inched toward her. It grinned, relishing her fear. But it didn't touch her, not yet. It made a gesture with one hand.

"No . . . no!" Madison cried. She was looking down at her own hand now, struggling, a pained expression on her face.

"What's happening?" Carmen shouted, wading back into the water after Bailee.

"I don't know," said Bailee with a shake of her head. She splashed farther into the river toward her friend.

"Give it to us," growled the second witch. It too had hauled itself out of the river, positioning itself on the rock next to the first. Together they loomed over Madison, whispering.

"No! Leave it alone," said Madison, voice shaking. She was still looking at her hands. As Bailee drew closer, she saw the focus of Madison's attention—the silver ring. It jumped and jostled against Madison's fumbling fingers.

All the while, the witches kept whispering.

Bailee finally understood. The witches were trying to snatch off Madison's ring. But why? Then she thought back to the evening of the play. When she'd presented the ring to Madison, she'd said it had a protection spell, one that would keep witches away. She understood now. The Specter was re-creating another one of her stories. As long as Madison wore the ring, the witches couldn't touch her.

"Hold on, Mads! I'm coming!" yelled Fen. He reached the flashlight and plucked it from the water. He turned the beam on the witches. But the light didn't stretch far enough. He let out a cry of frustration, racing toward Madison. But before he could reach her, he heard Madison scream in pain.

"Ow, ow, ow!" She yanked the ring from her finger as if it had burned her. It clattered onto the rock, glowing red-hot. Then, the ring flew up into the air. It landed in the outstretched hand of one of the witches.

At that moment the third, and final, witch appeared. It burst out of the water next to Madison. It cackled and grabbed hold of Madison's ringless hand.

"No!" Bailee shouted.

Madison collapsed.

The three witches howled with glee. Then before everyone's eyes they dissolved, twisting into tendrils of gray smoke. They streamed away downriver, out of sight.

In a blink the river calmed. The rushing waters receded. The stepping-stone bridge reappeared as if nothing out of the ordinary had happened. Bailee and Carmen scrambled onto the rocks and raced toward Madison.

"Is she okay?" Noah called from the river's edge. Beside him Abigail began to stir.

"More or less, I think," answered Carmen. Together she and Bailee helped Madison sit up, and they made their way toward the riverbank. Like Noah and Fen before, Madison wore a glazed, frightened expression. She moved like a sleepwalker, following Bailee and Carmen as they guided her across the stepping-stone rocks.

Fen joined them on the riverbank. He handed Carmen her flashlight.

"Still works," he said.

Carmen smiled. She looped her arm through the handle.

With Noah's help, Abigail was back on her feet now. "You okay?" he asked.

She waved him away impatiently. "I've been worse."

"That doesn't make you okay," said Carmen uneasily.

"I'll be fine. Just stretched a little thin right now," she said, her voice a hoarse whisper. "My powers—they're not as strong as the Specter's. It can recharge after just a few minutes, but I won't be back to full strength until the next game. Probably."

Bailee exchanged a worried look with her friends. Abigail was definitely looking less solid now, less real. At times it felt like Bailee could look right through their ghostly friend. Abigail said she'd be strong again when the game started up again next year, but what if she wasn't? Every encounter with the Specter left her a little more worn out, a little more lost. How much longer could she go on like this?

"We need to hurry. The Specter's getting stronger and stronger after each attack. It'll be back any moment," said Abigail, turning and walking upstream toward the bell.

Bailee couldn't help but notice how she wobbled unsteadily on her feet.

"You heard her. Follow that ghost," said Fen grimly. He gestured to Abigail.

They hurried after her with worry heavy in their stomachs.

CHAPTER 20
GREEN, GLITTERING LIGHT

They hugged the cliffs lining the river's edge, stumbling over slick rocks and fallen logs. Bailee kept a hand around Madison's waist, guiding her friend over the rough terrain, with Carmen helping from the other side. Madison murmured to herself as they went. Otherwise they walked in silence.

Overhead, light was fading fast. Deep shadows had settled in all around them. Bailee's eyes strained against the gloom, watching for signs of the Specter's return. The sounds of the rushing river and her own hammering heartbeat were loud in her ears. She shivered, only partly because her shoes and pants were soaked through. The longer the game went on, the more intense the Specter's attacks became. She noticed her friends throwing nervous glances over their

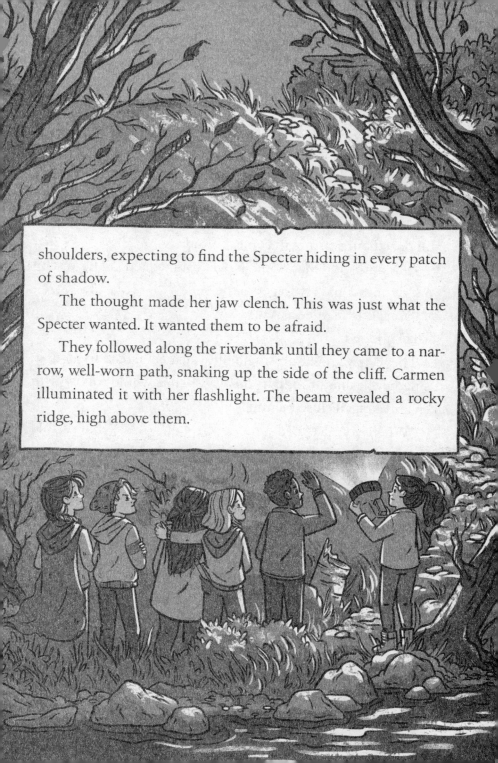

shoulders, expecting to find the Specter hiding in every patch of shadow.

The thought made her jaw clench. This was just what the Specter wanted. It wanted them to be afraid.

They followed along the riverbank until they came to a narrow, well-worn path, snaking up the side of the cliff. Carmen illuminated it with her flashlight. The beam revealed a rocky ridge, high above them.

"We'll climb up here," Abigail said. "The path continues above, winding along the ridge toward the falls. It'll take us to the bridge. The bell sits in a clearing just on the other side."

"Mads is still out of it," said Bailee. "She can walk okay, but I don't think she's up for climbing."

Madison muttered something from beside Bailee. She was still dazed but starting to come around.

"I'll stay with Madison," Noah volunteered. "The rest of you, go ahead and try to get to the bell."

"You sure?" Bailee asked.

He nodded.

They'd have to climb single file. Carmen agreed to go first, using her flashlight to light the way. Bailee would follow with Fen and Abigail close behind.

"When you get to the top, don't wait, okay?" Bailee told Carmen. "Just run for the bell. With your flashlight, you've got the best chance of winning. You've got this."

Carmen nodded nervously. She looped her arm through her flashlight's handle, and without another word, she started up the cliff. The beam of her flashlight bounced and swung in all directions as she climbed. Bailee started up after her, testing footholds and grabbing roots for support. She wouldn't be much use as a player if she fell and sprained an ankle. Or worse.

Carmen made it to the top. "The coast looks clear," she said, pulling herself up onto the ridge. She paused, scanning the path ahead with her flashlight. Then she screamed.

From below, the others watched as Carmen was pulled forward, out of sight. They heard her flashlight clatter to the ground and the ridge went dark.

"CARMEN!" Bailee shouted.

There was only a shriek of laughter in reply.

She scrambled up to the ridge with Abigail and Fen right behind. But when they reached the top, Carmen was nowhere to be found.

"CARMEN?" Bailee yelled again, searching.

"Where is she?" Fen said.

"There!" called Abigail. She pointed to a crumpled figure lying on the path ahead, just discernible in the gloom.

They ran over and crouched beside Carmen. Bailee brushed hair from Carmen's face. The girl's eyes were wide but unseeing.

"Where's her flashlight?" said Abigail. They searched the ground.

"This?" the Specter answered.

They turned.

A shadowy shape moved down the path toward them. With a click, Carmen's flashlight flared to life. But instead of its usual warm glow, it now shone a sickly green. The beam illuminated the Specter's Abigail-shaped face, shining under its chin like someone about to tell a ghost story.

"The flashlight," whispered Abigail, staring in horror.

A grin curled across the Specter's face. "Oh yes." It tossed the flashlight from one hand to the other. "This has been quite handy for you all tonight. But I'm afraid it's mine now."

"What do we do?" Fen asked.

"I don't know," Abigail answered.

"Looks like Carmen could use some help from her friends," said the Specter. "Oh, excuse me—you all aren't friends, not really. Before tonight, none of you spent more than five minutes with her outside of class. Isn't that right?"

Bailee felt a guilty twinge. It was no secret that Carmen

wasn't popular at school. And though she had never said anything bad about the girl, they had never been friends, either.

"Perfect, smarty-pants Carmen. That's what you all think, isn't it?" The Specter leered. "Useful if you need help with your homework or a quick answer in class to get the teacher off your back. But other than that, she might as well be invisible."

The Specter studied the flashlight. "What are the odds she'd bring this into the woods? One of the few objects with the power to keep me away. But Carmen's always had all the answers, hasn't she? Except for why no one likes her at school. She's been chasing the answer to that question for years. What is it about her, folks? Is it that she talks too much? Or not enough? Or that she'd rather study than go to the movies? Is it that she has to always be the smartest person in the room? That must be *so* annoying."

"Shut up!" Fen barked.

"Yeah, leave her alone," said Bailee.

"Hey now," the Specter protested. "This isn't me talking; it's Carmen. I can see into that mind of hers. *She's* the one who thinks everyone at school hates her. *She's* the one who thinks she's boring and predictable. *She's* the one who works and works and never feels good enough. *She's* the one who feels practically *invisible*." Its glittering eyes turned to Carmen. The Specter snapped its fingers.

"Oh no," Abigail whispered.

Bailee looked down. Her heart stopped.

Carmen had grown fuzzy around the edges. Bailee could make out the rocky contours of the ridge coming into clearer focus beneath Carmen's limp form. She was disappearing before their eyes, turning invisible.

"Stop!" Bailee cried. She and Fen crowded closer to Carmen, not knowing what to do. But the girl continued to fade.

"What?" the Specter snapped at them. "This is Carmen's story, remember? You two barely noticed her before tonight. She's felt invisible for years. It's not my fault you're only noticing now."

Bailee's face fell. Since the dare, she too had felt invisible. It was a terrible, lonely feeling, one she'd never suspected of the smartest kid in her class. Carmen had always looked so unbothered, so comfortable with not fitting in. But, Bailee supposed, it was hard to know what was really going on beneath the surface with people.

The Specter's face stretched into a dramatic yawn. "Ugh . . . self-doubt. Maybe Carmen's right. She *could* be a little more exciting. Even her scary story is dull."

"SHUT UP!" Fen yelled again, louder.

The Specter's glittering gaze turned to the boy. Its Abigail-shaped mouth curled into a grin. "Not a fan of Carmen's story? Can't relate? Hmm . . . perhaps this one will hit closer to home?"

The Specter opened its mouth, but the voice that came out was different than usual. *"You'd better shape up, Fen! You're going nowhere with this attitude of yours. Is that where you want to end up? Nowhere? At this point the only thing you're good at is screwing up!"*

Fen flinched away. The color drained from his face.

The Specter doubled over with laughter. "Thought that might hit a nerve."

Bailee and Abigail looked at Fen, a mixture of concern and confusion on their faces. But there was no time for questions.

The Specter walked toward them holding Carmen's flashlight in its pale hands. As it drew near, the beam began to flicker. Then, like a candle snuffed out by the wind, the flashlight died.

Darkness settled in all around them, choking and heavy.

Night had come. The moon had yet to rise above the trees. The forest was a mass of murky grays.

Bailee inched backward. She felt Fen and Abigail beside her. The Specter stood before them, just a shifting smudge against the gloom. They might not have known it was there at all if not for its glittering eyes.

"Do you know why humans are afraid of the dark?" the Specter said thoughtfully. It tucked Carmen's flashlight away under its cloak. "It's not the dark they fear. It's what might be lurking *in* the dark that makes people tremble. They're afraid of the unseen. The unknown. Humans, you see, are not blessed with extraordinary sight. They do, however, have wonderful imaginations. And nothing sets the human mind imagining like the unknown. Or the dark."

Leaves rustled as the Specter took a step forward. Bailee, Abigail, and Fen tensed, ready to run.

The Specter giggled. "It's silly, really. The dark can't hurt you. But I can. Especially with my new trick." The Specter pushed back its hood.

Bailee, Abigail, and Fen gasped in shock.

The Specter had begun to glow. Light radiated from its hands and face as if lit from within by a strange green fire. Its eyes blazed, brighter than ever before.

The Specter might have been underwhelmed by Carmen's story, but her gift had left it transformed.

"How—" Bailee looked to Abigail.

"I—I don't know," she said. "This has never happened before." Green light reflected in her wide, frightened eyes.

The Specter was speaking again. "Lurking in the shadows has always been very effective for me. The human mind is so good at conjuring horrors, and I'm happy to snatch them away." The Specter giggled again, advancing on them. "But I always thought *seeing* was far scarier than imagining. Because when you imagine, there's always the possibility that what you fear isn't real. But when you see it . . . well, what do you think?" It sneered at them like a horrible nightlight.

Bailee's mind whirred. With the Specter no longer afraid of the light, they had no way to protect themselves. Her eyes traveled along the narrow ridge and up the path ahead. She could hear the rush of the falls in the distance. The bell was so close. But the Specter blocked her way.

She inched backward again, away from the Specter's terrible jack-o'-lantern grin. Her foot edged off the path, sending rocks and dirt tumbling down the steep slope of the ridge behind her. The river swirled below.

They were trapped.

"It's your turn, Bailee. Time to tell me your story. Hand over your journal, and I'll let you go home safe and sound. Of course, once I win the game, the same cannot be said for your town. And with my new power, think of the damage I'll do." The Specter flexed its glowing fingers. "No more hiding from the light for me. I can stroll into town in broad daylight now if I want. What fun that will be."

Any plan that had started to formulate in Bailee's head was overtaken by panic as the Specter took another step toward her. She couldn't get away, not this time. She was the only player left. Winning the game was all on her now. But there was no way she could do this on her own.

Suddenly Noah and Madison were there. Breathing hard, they crowded in front of Bailee, shielding her from the Specter. Fen and Abigail stepped up to join them. They kept their eyes on the Specter, but Madison's hand found Bailee's. Bailee felt hope spark inside. Her friend might not have been there for her after the dare, but she was here now. Bailee didn't have to do this alone.

The Specter laughed.

"Nice try, but there are limits to the protection your sacrificed gifts offer." Its eyes glittered menacingly at Bailee's friends.

"We're not going anywhere," said Fen stubbornly.

"Yeah, not until we've done everything we can to stop you," said Noah. Madison nodded.

The Specter smirked. "Such brave pals you have, Bailee. But it's no use. The game is mine."

The Specter took a step toward them.

"Bailee," Fen whispered.

"Yeah?" she whispered back, eyes wide with panic.

"Get ready to run."

Then, with a yell, Fen flew at the Specter. He caught it around the waist. Together they fell in a heap on the ground.

"Go!" Fen shouted, and then his face went blank. He collapsed.

CHAPTER 21
THE DEEP, DEEP DOWN

Bailee didn't need to be told twice. She skirted around Fen and the Specter and bolted down the ridge toward the falls and the bell.

"YES! GO, BAILEE!" yelled Madison.

"RUN!" cried Noah.

The Specter sat up, pushing Fen's unconscious form away. "Your gift may keep the rest of your stories safe from me tonight, but you aren't immune

to my touch," it said, laughing at Fen's lifeless form. It scrambled to its feet. Madison, Noah, and Abigail rushed to block its way, but the Specter only laughed again. Then it began writhing and twisting, shifting shape. It dissolved and re-formed before them. The wolf-monster snapped and snarled at them now. It let out an earsplitting howl, then leaped over them and launched itself after Bailee.

She ran as fast as she could, following the winding ridge. The sound of the rushing water told her she was drawing close to Silver Falls. Soon she spotted the bridge in the distance. It stretched out in front of her, coming closer with each step. Something glinted in the darkness just beyond. The bell.

The Specter was howling with glee now, chasing after Bailee in its wolf form. "Yes, run! It's so much fun when you run!"

Bailee's feet found the bridge. The wooden boards were slick, wet from the waterfall's billowing mist. Between the slats of the boards, she could see the Hollow River frothing far below. The sight made her stomach turn. She fixed her eyes on the bell and kept running.

With a leap, the Specter soared over Bailee's head. It landed on the far side of the bridge with a crash. The whole structure lurched as if it were about to shake apart. The Specter-wolf snarled at Bailee.

She tried to stop, but her feet slid over the slick boards. They came out from under her, and she landed hard. Her journal shook loose from her waistband. Bailee stretched an arm out after it but not in time. She watched in horror as it skipped out of reach, sailed under the bottommost rail, and dropped out of sight. It was gobbled up by the river below.

The Specter howled and stamped its paws with delight. It dissolved like smoke, reappearing again as a nightmare version of Abigail. It loomed over Bailee.

"Oops, looks like you've dropped your book of stories." Its Abigail-shaped face stretched into a grin. "It's not wise to be without a gift in this game. Without anything to sacrifice, I can just take, take, *take*." The Specter stepped forward, stretching a glowing green hand toward Bailee.

She yelped, jerking away. But the movement carried her too far. Her legs shot out below the bottom rail. She wedged her fingers between the boards and held on tight. Below her dangling feet, the Hollow River swirled, eager to swallow her up, just like her journal.

Then Abigail—the real one—was there.

She dashed across the bridge and grabbed onto Bailee's hand, trying to haul her back up to safety.

"It's too late, Abby," growled the Specter. "The game's over." It lunged for Bailee.

Abigail threw herself in front of the Specter. It grazed the girl's arm. She dropped like a stone.

"Abigail!" Bailee cried as the other girl tumbled headfirst from the bridge. Bailee managed to grab Abigail's arm with one hand. But the weight of both of them was too much.

They fell.

They plunged into the river. The shock of the icy water drove the breath from Bailee's lungs. She thrashed and struggled, but the strong current dragged her downward, as if she were nothing more than a soggy leaf. She twisted and tumbled, unable to tell which way was up.

She stuck out an arm, then winced as her elbow collided with a rock. She pushed away only to strike another. It raked her side, and she cried out. Bubbles escaped from her mouth, and earthy river water flooded in.

Real terror seized her then, worse than anything she had felt so far that night.

She was going to drown.

She squinted her eyes open, searching desperately for the surface. But murky gloom was all she could see. Then a shimmer caught her eye. Bailee didn't know what it was, but she pushed toward it, reaching. Warmth suddenly blossomed in her fingertips, and the pain in her lungs began to ease. The warmth traveled up her arms and through her body. She wasn't struggling against the current anymore. She wasn't in the river at all.

She was running.

She felt her feet slap against hard earth. Tall trees pressed in close around her as she barreled headlong down a winding path through the woods. Thunder boomed overhead, but it was a faraway sound, muffled by a strange rushing in Bailee's ears. She sprinted through the forest. She felt fear pulsing inside her, but it wasn't her own. Whatever was happening, she wasn't in control. She was only along for the ride.

She came to a steep embankment and began to scrabble up. Suddenly she went sprawling.

A hand had grabbed her ankle.

Bailee turned and found herself face-to-face with another girl, one about her age. Bailee felt a flicker of familiarity. Did she know this person?

She squirmed, and the other girl's face twisted into a vicious sneer, eyes shining. A hand reached for Bailee's neck.

Bailee felt herself kick, catching the girl in her shoulder.

Then the world around her skipped. It was like a jolt in her stomach, a sensation like missing a step in the dark. Suddenly, Bailee found herself peering over a rocky ledge. Below, the girl from before paced up and down the forest path with two other kids by her side. A small silver locket dangled from the girl's hand.

That's mine, thought Bailee. Then she corrected herself. No, the locket wasn't hers. It belonged to the same person who owned the fear she felt pulsing alongside her own.

Without warning, there was a flash of light overhead.

She flinched away, whirling around. Then she saw something that made her gasp.

A shadowy figure loomed over her, one with glittering green eyes. It stretched out a hand, reaching for her.

She stumbled back, away from the thing. Then there was no ground beneath her. For the second time that day, she was falling.

Her world skipped again.

Bailee opened her eyes and found herself standing in the hallway of a school—her school, she realized. The lockers were a different color, but the floor tiles were the same. Shinier and less scuffed, but the same. She was carrying a stack of books in her arms, a mix of textbooks and novels. Bailee studied the covers. They had names like *The Mystery at McNaughton Manor* and *The Clue Behind the Mirror*. Whoever she was riding along with now was a big mystery fan.

Unfamiliar faces streamed by her. Suddenly there was a sharp pain in her shin. She tumbled to the ground. Her books crashed to the floor.

"Oops!" came a voice.

Bailee's head turned in time to catch the speaker.

It was the girl from the woods.

"Sorry! Didn't see you there." The girl smirked, then disappeared into the crowd.

Bailee felt her face grow hot. Careless, sneakered feet stomped her fingers as she tried to gather her books.

Skip.

Bailee was in a classroom now, sitting at a desk. A teacher walked the aisles. Bailee saw a sheet of paper land on her desk—a test. Fractions.

Bailee groaned. But she didn't have to take the test. It was already done. A large A-plus sat in the top corner.

"Excellent work as always," said the teacher as she passed. "If I'm not careful, you'll be taking my job soon."

Bailee felt an inward glow, an unusual feeling for her in math class. A part of her loved the idea of teaching math—the part of Bailee that wasn't *her*.

Skip.

She was in a semi-dark room now. A bedroom. She lay in a slender bed. On the opposite wall, sunrise peeked in around the curtains hanging in the window. In the far corner Bailee spied a small dresser with a mirror hanging just above. A tiny desk, stacked high with books, was crammed into another corner. A thin stream of light slanted across the floor from the open doorway. She felt herself push the covers back and walk over to the dresser, peering into the mirror.

Bailee gasped. The face staring back at her wasn't her own. It was Abigail's.

The door pushed open. A wet, black nose and two soft brown eyes greeted her. A wagging tail followed. A dog stood in the doorway, wriggling with delight.

"Good morning, Elvis. Are you the best boy or what?" Bailee heard Abigail's voice say. She knelt, and the dog licked her face in response. Bailee felt a surge of love course through her.

Skip.

Outside this time, walking through the woods. It was coming on night. She was bundled in a winter coat. Her breath plumed out in front of her like clouds. All was silent and still. As she walked, snow began to fall. Big, fluffy flakes. Bailee felt herself take a deep breath in and let it out slowly, savoring the faint scent of chimney smoke edging the crisp air.

It was a peaceful moment but mixed with a hint of longing. *If only I had someone to share this with*, she thought.

Skip.

Skip.

Skip.

The moments came fast now and picked up more speed. Bailee felt as if she were caught in a tornado as chaotic scenes whirled all around. Some were quiet, others loud. Some rang with laughter, and others left her sick with worry or embarrassment. She caught snatches of conversation, faces, and images. She began to feel dizzy. If only she could grab hold of one of these moments—no, not moments. Memories.

She reached out a grasping hand, willing the whirlwind of scenes and emotions to slow.

To her surprise, she felt another hand grab hold of her own. She was pulled through the swirling storm of memories, back into the cold rush of the river.

CHAPTER 22
WHERE MEMORIES GO

Bailee coughed and spluttered as her head broke the surface.

The hand holding hers was Abigail's. Together they half swam, half stumbled toward the riverbank.

The current had brought them to a calm, shallow spot downriver. They clambered onto a low, sandy bank. Beside them the forest rose up sharply and a high cliff towered over them, blending with the night sky above. Bailee didn't know for sure, but she guessed they were far from the falls and the bell now. But at least they were safe.

"Th-th-th-thanks," Bailee said, teeth chattering from the cold. Water dripped from her hair and ran down her face. She squeezed the sleeves of her jacket and sweater, but it was no use; she was hopelessly soaked.

The moon peeked over the trees, round and orange like a pumpkin. It spilled warm light onto the river. Abigail crouched on the bank next to Bailee, curled into a small ball. She was also soaked through, but the cold didn't appear to bother her. If there was any doubt about Abigail being a ghost before, there wasn't anymore. She was a wisp of her former self now, and Bailee could see right through her. The look in Abigail's eyes was distant, as if she had retreated inside herself. Whatever power was responsible for making Abigail solid during the game, it was almost used up.

Bailee watched the river lapping at Abigail's feet. Perhaps another aspect of the game was wearing her thin too.

"I'm guessing you saw," said Abigail, voice small. She gestured to the river.

"It was the Specter," Bailee said. "The day you died—it was watching you in the woods. It was trying to catch you. But before it could, you fell from the ridge. You drowned in the river. . . ."

Abigail nodded.

"Is—is that why you're still here? Why you're brought back for the game?" Bailee asked.

"I don't know," said Abigail, sounding tired. "Maybe my death created some sort of loophole in the game; I never rang the bell. But I didn't leave the woods either. The power at work here is far older than me. I doubt anyone truly understands it."

Bailee looked at the river. "I saw other things too. Were they . . . your memories?"

Abigail nodded again. "I never had anything to give the Specter, no gift to sacrifice in exchange for safe passage out of the woods. So it's found other things to take—my memories. I think the Specter keeps them here in the river to taunt me. Close enough to touch but impossible to hold." She reached into the river, cupping water in her ghostly hand. She watched as it slowly drained away. "I think the Specter likes to remind me of where my old life ended . . . and where my new existence began."

"That's why your mind slips, isn't it?" Bailee felt anger flare. "That's why you have such difficulty remembering? The Specter's been stealing your memories away. For years!"

Abigail nodded. "It wasn't so bad at first. It only took the most painful ones. Those are basically scary stories, right? Ones we replay in our minds over and over. I didn't mind giving those up. I mean, it's bad enough being dead, but having an eternity to dwell on all your unhappiest moments? No thanks." Abigail's mouth twitched into a grim smile. "But the Specter didn't stop at the bad memories. After a while it took whatever it could. I started to forget everything—where I grew up, what my house looked like, who my parents were. Sometimes I feel like I barely know who I am anymore. It's like the Specter is more *me* than—well, me." Abigail squeezed her eyes shut, looking frailer than ever. "I try to be more careful these days. Keep away from the Specter so I can hold on to what I have left. But it hasn't been easy."

Bailee shook her head. "You can't go on like this. Running from the Specter, sacrificing more and more of yourself each time you're caught. Soon you'll have nothing left. You . . . You won't even remember who you are!"

"What else can I do?" said Abigail, anger sparking behind her eyes now. "Just sit back and watch? Just let the Specter win and terrorize the town for a whole year, growing stronger and more unstoppable? I don't think so. When kids need my help, I help, even if that means I'm a little less *me* afterward. Because when they win the game, the Specter rests. The town is safe. And I finally get some peace . . . at least for a little while, until the game starts up again."

"But even if we win tonight, what about the kids next year, and the years after that? They'll come into the woods, and the Specter will hunt them down, terrifying them with their own awful stories, just like it did to us. We're lucky no one's been seriously hurt tonight! And that's only because we had you to help us. Things can't continue like this. It's not safe. For anyone!" Bailee's hands trembled, partly from the cold and partly out of anger. "There has to be something else we can do. Something to not just end the game tonight, but forever."

"I wish there were" said Abigail sadly. She stood up, gazing out over the river. Her eyes had grown distant, and a crease formed in the middle of her brow. Her mind had slipped again—lost.

Bailee bit back her frustration. Abigail was trying her best to help them. Like Bailee and her friends, she was playing by rules she didn't fully understand. It wasn't fair. There had to be something they could do to help her. But what?

Bailee reached for her journal, but then she remembered—it was gone, lost to the river. She stared helplessly at the river, shivering violently. Her throat squeezed with fear. Here she was, soaked to the bone, stranded in the dark, and her only company was a ghost who couldn't remember who she was for more than a few minutes at a time. Not to mention she had just lost her only protection from the Specter.

Bailee drew her knees to her chest and wrapped her arms around them. Her teeth chattered. She'd felt alone plenty of times in her life, especially during the past few weeks. But she was *really* alone now. Just when she needed help the most.

Then she heard familiar voices. They were close. And coming closer.

"Hello?" Bailee called. She stood, searching for movement up on the dark cliffs lining the river's edge.

"Bailee!" Madison's voice called back.

Bailee heard the sound of rustling branches high above. Then Madison's voice again. "They're here! They're all right!"

"Thank goodness!" Carmen cried.

"Weird time for a swim!" called Fen from somewhere in the gloom. Bailee couldn't make out his expression, but she imagined him smirking.

"Yeah, stop wasting time, you two," Noah joked. "We have to finish the game!"

Bailee's blue lips stretched into a smile.

CHAPTER 23
THE PLAN

Noah acted as an anchor, bracing himself against a tree. Then, arms interlocked to form a human chain, he, Fen, Madison, and Carmen hoisted Bailee and Abigail up the steep slope of the cliff.

As soon as they were on flat ground, Madison flew at Bailee, almost sending them both tumbling. She wrapped her soggy friend in a tight hug.

"Can't. Breathe." Bailee pretended to choke even as she hugged Madison back.

Madison laughed, eyes shining. "Deal with it. I thought I was never going to see you again. Are you okay?" She stepped back to inspect.

"Fine. Abigail saved me. But I wish I had a towel." Bailee's teeth chattered again.

"Abigail, are you all right?" Noah studied her with concern.

"Pretty much the same as always," Abigail said with a weak smile. But anyone who looked at her knew this wasn't true. She was almost invisible now. They could barely make her out in the thin moonlight. It was clear that whatever power brought Abigail back during the game was almost used up.

"Is everyone else okay? Carmen?" Bailee asked. She turned to the girl. Carmen looked smaller without her flashlight.

"Um . . . it took a few minutes to come around, but I'm okay. Feeling a bit embarrassed . . . Noah and Madison told me what happened." Carmen shifted from one foot to the other.

"You've got nothing to be embarrassed about," said Madison.

Noah nodded.

"Yeah, no one in the Specter Survivors' Club should ever feel embarrassed," added Fen.

Carmen nodded, looking a little brighter.

"Fen? You okay?" Bailee asked.

"Can't say I'm a fan of being knocked out twice in one night, but could be worse." He rubbed his forehead.

"We were worried about you two," said Noah, nodding at Bailee and Abigail.

"I don't know what I would have done if you'd been hurt," said Madison, voice choked. "I'm so sorry, Bailee—for everything. I had no idea what would happen when I told

Bright about Fen's dare. I didn't want one of my friends getting hurt. But I ended up hurting another friend instead."

"It's okay, Mads," Bailee said. "It was absolutely the right call to tell someone about the dare. I just wish you had told *me* that you had."

"I wish I had too."

Bailee drew Madison into another hug. She didn't need to hear more. She knew Madison hadn't meant to hurt her. Bailee had gotten the truth and an apology. And her best friend back.

"I hate to spoil a happy moment, but we still need a plan to get past the Specter," said Noah.

"Lucky for you, plans are Madison's specialty," said Bailee.

Madison gave her friend one last squeeze, then gathered the others and began strategizing.

Bailee took off her soaked jacket and sweater and hung them on a low-hanging branch. Shivering in just her T-shirt, she rang out her sopping clothes. The icy water made her fingers sting. Her teeth chattered worse than ever.

"Here," said Fen. He shrugged off his hoodie and held it out toward her.

Bailee felt another wave of goose bumps cascade down her arms. She took the sweatshirt from him. "Thanks," she said, pulling it over her head. It was warm and dry. "And thanks for what you did back there, tackling the Specter."

"No problem. And I'm . . . I wanted to say . . . I'm sorry too. About all the stuff with the dare. I didn't know it was Madison who told, and even if I did, I shouldn't have been so mad." He stared hard at the ground. "Mads was just trying to keep me from breaking my neck. I get that now. I guess I was just mad because . . ." He paused.

Bailee didn't say anything, just listened.

Fen took a deep breath. "Things have been kind of rough at home lately," he said finally. "My dad hasn't been able to find a job since the factory shut down, and he's—he's sort of been taking it out on my mom and me. Always shouting at us and stuff." Fen's voice grew hard and bitter.

Bailee's eyes went wide. She reached for Fen. "Are you okay? What's been going on?" Her dad used to work at the same factory as Mr. Leer before it closed. The past two years had definitely been rough for Bailee's dad, bouncing from job to job. Her whole family had felt the stress. She'd imagined Fen's family was having similar problems. But she never imagined anything like this.

Fen held his hands up in a calming gesture. "It's okay. We're okay. At least, we are now. We're staying with my aunt for a while. Things have been better since we moved. A lot better. But . . . I guess I haven't really been dealing with it. Not well, anyway. Then the dare happened and I got suspended, and everyone was saying it was your fault. It was just easier to take out everything I was feeling on you. And that wasn't fair."

Bailee stared wide-eyed at Fen. "You're sure you're okay?"

He nodded. "Yeah. And I'm sorry."

Bailee was quiet for a moment. "Thanks," she said finally. "For telling me all that. And for saying sorry. I'm sorry too. I wish I had known things weren't okay with you. I wish I could have—"

"You didn't know." Fen shrugged. "Mads does. We've talked about it a bit, when I moved into my aunt's place. But with the dare and stuff at school, I didn't get the chance to tell you. . . ."

"I understand. I'm glad I know now," Bailee said.

They exchanged small smiles. Bailee knew things weren't all fixed between them, not yet, but this was a good start.

She wrung more water out of her hair, and then she and Fen joined the others. Madison had taken charge. She was drawing a rough map of their location in the dirt with a stick, like a general preparing troops for battle.

We'll be approaching from the opposite side of the river now.

Near the bridge is a clearing.

That's where the bell is.

"We'll have to be on alert, though. In the dark we're practically sitting ducks for the Specter," Madison finished.

"There's one more problem," Bailee added. "I lost my journal. My gift. It's somewhere downriver now."

Noah groaned. "I wanted to read that."

"The real problem is, without a gift, Bailee has no protection from the Specter. It'll be free to take whatever it wants from her, as many times as it can catch her," said Abigail, eyes tired and hollow.

"Bailee's brain is like a treasure trove of spooky stuff too," said Madison with a shiver. "A lot of potential stories for the Specter to use for years to come."

"I always knew your horror fixation would cause trouble." Fen shot Bailee a grim smile.

No one spoke for a moment.

"We need a diversion of some sort," Carmen said finally.

"I could distract the Specter," said Fen. "I could tackle it again and buy Bailee some time."

But Abigail shook her head. "The Specter knows it's close to winning the game. It'll be focused on Bailee, no one else."

"There's got to be something else we can do," said Noah, thinking out loud. "Some other sort of diversion."

"Too bad we don't have the Specter's powers," said Carmen.

"Yeah, Bailee could morph into a ghost or something and just blow right by the Specter," Fen said.

Bailee nodded. "The power to shape-shift would be handy right now. Being anyone, or *anything*, other than myself right now is just what we need."

Madison paused as if a light bulb had just flicked on in her mind. Her eyes darted around her circle of friends. They stopped on Bailee, still wearing Fen's sweater.

The Plan

"We don't have the Specter's power of disguise," Madison said, "but I think I know the next best thing."

They moved as quickly as they could through the dark woods, pushing through bushes and stumbling over felled trees. The thunder of the falls grew louder as they went, signaling they were closing in on the bell.

"Okay, everyone, remember the plan," Madison whispered from somewhere in the gloom. "Hoods up!"

One by one, Bailee and her friends drew up the hoods of their jackets and sweaters. They cinched the drawstrings tight, securing them in place. Then they picked up the pace.

Soon the ground around them flattened and the trees thinned. A broad clearing stretched out before them, awash in moonlight. It was a space roughly the size of Beckett's junior soccer field, with tall trees ringing the edges. On the farthest side, near the falls, sat the bell. Moonlight caught on its jagged, weather-worn lip, glinting, calling them forward.

"Next phase!" shouted Madison. "Run!"

Six hooded figures broke from the trees, sprinting across the clearing toward the bell. Bailee kept to the side closest to the river, weaving between trees along the cliff's edge. Abigail sprinted along the opposite edge of the clearing, where the forest grew thick and wild. The others ran up the middle. No one spoke. The only sound was the crunch of their footsteps and the shiver of the leaves in the trees.

Then a strange noise met their ears.

"I don't like the sound of that," Noah puffed as he ran.

Bailee heard it too. An ominous creaking followed by a strange ripping sound.

"It's coming from the woods!" Fen yelled.

"Ignore it. Keep running!" Abigail said.

Bailee kept her focus on the bell. She could see it clearly now, almost glowing in the moonlight. She willed her legs to move faster.

Then she caught something out of the corner of her eye. She heard Abigail cry out.

In the forest beside her, branches shook. Trees swayed. It looked as if something huge moved within, pushing to get out. But it wasn't some strange creature. It was the trees. They were moving on their own.

"Yikes!" yelled Madison. She and the others stumbled to a stop.

Trees marched out of the forest and into the clearing—short, shaggy cedars; elegant oaks; and towering sycamores. Branches

thrashed and roots flailed like strange tentacles, propelling the trees onward, inch by inch. They were coming right at Bailee and her friends. Then the whispers started.

Get them. Get them. Get them.

It was the trees; their cones and sparse leaves rustled in their branches, whispering the words.

"Okay, the *actual* forest is chasing us now!" yelled Noah. He took off running with Abigail and Carmen close behind. Suddenly, a root sprung from the ground in front of him. Noah's foot connected with it. He stumbled but recovered his balance and kept running.

CRAAAACK!

It was a sound like a massive bone breaking in two. Carmen, Noah, and Fen skidded to a stop just as an enormous tree toppled from the woods, directly in their path.

More trees began to topple and fall. Madison and Abigail dodged one as it fell in front of them.

CRACK! CRACK! CRACK! The earth shook with each impact as more trees toppled to the ground.

Get them! Get them! The whispering from the trees grew louder.

"Phase three, now!" shouted Madison, her voice shrill with fear.

Just like they had planned, two of them broke from the group and bolted for the bell. Bailee was one of them. Her hood was drawn up tight, hiding her face. The rest of the group followed, cheering. But their cries of excitement soon turned to dismay.

A root burst from the ground, springing up like a snare.

"Oof!" came the voice from under Bailee's hood. She went down, hard. More roots sprang from the earth, sending clumps of dirt into the air. They latched on to her arms and legs, holding her fast.

Then Noah yelped. Carmen, Madison, and Fen did too. More roots burst from the ground and wrapped tightly around their ankles and wrists. One by one they fell. They struggled against their root bindings, but it was no use. They were trapped.

A shriek of glee erupted from the woods. The Specter emerged. It glowed bright green with its new power, stolen from Carmen's flashlight.

"Bailee, nice to see you!" Its not-quite-Abigail face sneered as it walked over to her prone figure, lashed to the forest floor. It stretched out a pale arm, one finger extended. "Tag . . .," it said.

"You're still it," an unexpected voice answered, coming from within Bailee's hood.

The Specter drew back in surprise. With a flick of its wrist, a root leaped from the ground and snatched the hood from Bailee's head. Except it wasn't Bailee.

It was Abigail.

CHAPTER 24
ABIGAIL'S LAST STAND

"Like looking in the worst mirror," Abigail wheezed. Her breaths came in shallow gasps. She glared at the mottled, green-glowing version of herself that was the Specter.

"If you're here, where's . . . ?" it snarled, eyes darting around the clearing. Then it saw what it was looking for.

A figure in a red cloak sprinted along the edge of the cliff, just a flickering shadow under the cover of darkness. The hood drawn up over the figure's head fell back to reveal who it was.

"RUN, BAILEE! GO!" yelled Madison.

The Specter shrieked with fury.

Bailee's teeth chattered and her soaked jeans clung to her legs as she ran, but a smile curled on her face. The plan was working! She flew as fast as she could, each step closing the gap between the bell and her. She locked her eyes on the bell's pull rope, swaying in the breeze. She stretched out a hand, ready to grab it. It was just a stone's throw away now.

At that moment a leafy maple tree knocked her off her feet.

Bailee cried out. She fell to her hands and knees. Then she felt the ground slope away beneath her. The force of the collision had sent her over the cliff's edge. She tumbled head over heels down the steep slope toward the river. Her hands clawed at dirt and stones, trying to catch hold of something. But it was no use. Finally she slammed into a large rock protruding from the ground. She let out a weak cry, then was still.

For a moment Bailee didn't move. Finally, she opened her eyes with a groan. The woods swam around her. She staggered to her feet, ears ringing. She knew she had to get to the bell. But which direction was it? Before she could get her bearings, something rough grabbed her by the arm.

"Ow!" Bailee yelped. Thin, rough branches like long fingers twined around her stomach, arms, and legs. They hoisted her into the air. Soon Bailee was face-to-face with a monstrous, scowling maple tree.

Get the girl. Stop the girl. Bring the girl, leaves whispered all around her.

Bailee struggled and kicked, but the branches only gripped more tightly. The maple tucked her under one limb as if she weighed no more than a piece of split firewood. It marched her up the cliff's slope and across the clearing toward the Specter's beckoning glow.

"C'mon!" Bailee moaned as she wriggled against the tree's suffocating grasp. "Don't let the Specter tell you what to do! I always assumed maple trees were sweet." But the tree continued as if it hadn't heard. Maybe trees didn't have ears.

The Specter slow-clapped as Bailee and her leafy captor shuddered to a halt before it. "What fun! So few think of such exciting distractions. But I'm afraid you came up short. Now, as exhilarating as this all has been," the Specter growled, "it's time to tell me your story."

A pale, glowing hand reached for Bailee. She kicked and fought, trying to push herself as far away from the Specter's reaching fingers as she could.

"Let her go," Abigail said. The ghostly girl rose from the ground, straining against the roots holding her captive. She squeezed her eyes shut and summoned what was left of her power. One by one the roots wrapped around her arms and legs fell away. She staggered to her feet.

The Specter snapped its fingers. More roots sprang up, but

Abigail held out her hands, making them fall to the ground, lifeless. She was breathing hard, near exhaustion, but she staggered toward Bailee and the Specter.

"Come on, Abby," the Specter said. "Forget these kids. Stop playing for the losing team."

"My name is *Abigail*. I hate being called Abby—at least, I think I do. . . ." Abigail bit her lip. Uncertainty clouded in her eyes. Her mind was slipping again. She fought to keep her thoughts together.

"Abby, these kids—they don't care about you. Year after year is the same; they come into the woods, play the game, and then leave you behind. They go home and spread all those nasty stories. Terrible stories. *Monstrous* stories. All about you."

"It's not their fault. They just don't know. They don't remember . . . ," said Abigail, sounding less firm. "Besides, it doesn't matter. Their stories aren't true. I'm not a monster. I know and that's enough. It should be enough. . . ." Her expression went hazy.

"You don't need to fight it, Abby," the Specter growled. "Embrace what they say. You've only had a taste of the power that lives in these woods. But you could have more. You know, we could share the power, Abby. Like friends. That's what you really want, isn't it? Friends. That's *really* why you help these kids year after year." The Specter grinned. "Poor, lonely Abby. The kids—they don't understand. But I do. I know what it's like to be lonely. But if we played the game together, we wouldn't have to be lonely anymore."

Abigail backed away, shaking her head. "No, it's not right. *I don't want to be like you.*"

"But you're fading, Abby. You must feel it. Your power is almost all used up. And your remaining memories? They're almost all gone too. It won't be long until you're lost altogether. No one will remember who you were. Not even you."

"That's not true!" said Noah. He kicked against the roots holding him. "We know who you are! You're not like the Specter. We'll remember—"

"Not tomorrow, you won't," the Specter snarled.

"Don't listen, Abigail! It's just using you!" cried Madison.

"And how is that different from what any of you have done?" The Specter's voice was a cold, cutting wind now. "You think I don't know what you wanted when you stepped into the woods this evening? All your minds are open books to me." It shoved a finger in Madison's face. "You, Miss Keeper, were happy enough to use the game to make yourself popular. Hashtag Abigail Snook, right? You didn't care if the stories about Abigail were true or not. As long as the game you organized was a success. As long as it made *you* a success."

Madison's face fell.

"Hey—" started Fen. But the Specter rounded on him.

"And you? You didn't care what went on in the woods. The game was just another risk you couldn't resist. You can't help but live down to everyone's expectations. All you're good at is screwing up—isn't that so, Fen?"

Fen glared at the Specter, then looked away.

It turned to Carmen. "And let's not stop there! You wanted to show you were more than just a smarty-pants. More than just Carmen, the walking search engine. Maybe if people saw *fun* Carmen, the Carmen that would risk a night in the woods with Abigail Snook, they'd want to be friends—isn't that right?"

Carmen scowled at the Specter. "Your speculations are specious at best."

"And the journalist over there?" The Specter pointed at Noah. "He was going to use Abigail as his first feature story. Redeem himself after his last article at his old school was a big old flop and he lost all his friends. Who needs pals anyway, when you've got a story to chase? Right, Noah?"

"It's not like that—" Noah shook his head.

"Then there's our little storyteller here. You're worst of all," the Specter continued, turning finally to Bailee. A wicked smile spread across its Abigail-shaped face. "Yes, I know what was in that journal of yours, all those stories about Abigail. You hardly cared if they were true. You only cared about what made for the best scary story. That's why you're here— you wanted to live out your own spooky tale. You wanted to find out what *really* went on in the Bellwoods on Halloween night."

Bailee felt her face grow hot.

"But that's not all, is it? You *needed* to win the game. You couldn't wait to see the looks on your classmates' faces when you came out of the woods, Bellwoods Game winner. They'd have a much harder time ignoring you after that, wouldn't they? Maybe they'd even like you again. No more Bailee the outcast—that's what you hoped. And how lucky you were to have Abigail here to help you."

Bailee's fists clenched, but she said nothing.

"See? Nothing to say. We all wanted our own little piece of Abigail. We all used her. At least I'm honest about it," said the Specter with a sniff.

Abigail looked around at them all, fresh hurt in her eyes. She flickered a little, looking like the flame of a candle about to burn out. But Bailee couldn't let that happen. What the Specter said wasn't wrong, but it also wasn't the full story.

"Abigail," she cried, struggling against the tree's grasp. "I'm sorry for what happened to you all those years ago. And I'm sorry for what people have said, what *we've all said* about you."

Abigail's eyes met Bailee's. She flickered again.

"You're more than this game." Bailee's words spilled out. "I saw your memories in the river. I know you loved to read. Mysteries were your favorite."

Abigail looked at Bailee, unsure. Then she nodded slowly, remembering.

"And you were great at math," Bailee continued. "You wanted to be a teacher when you grew up, right?"

Abigail nodded again. She wasn't flickering anymore. She was still transparent but growing solid—more real looking—with each word Bailee spoke.

"Hey, now . . . ," the Specter started, but Bailee kept going.

"You had a dog named Elvis. You loved him so much. Do you remember?"

"Elvis." Abigail nodded, face stretching with sudden joy. "I remember. Of course I do." Abigail looked almost normal now. Every memory Bailee gave her was like kindling feeding Abigail's fragile fire.

"You've got something nice to say about everyone, even Mr. Owens and his weird stories," said Fen, catching on. "Did he ever tell you the one about how his garden gnome was supposedly playing tricks on him?"

Abigail grinned, turning to him. "Yeah, I remember that one now."

"That's enough!" the Specter shouted.

"You helped us find Carmen after she got lost!" yelled Noah, drowning out the Specter's whine.

"And you kept us all from getting crushed in the cut," Carmen added.

"You saved Bailee from drowning in the river," said Madison. "I'll never forget that; no *way* this game can wipe that from my mind."

"You're better than this." Bailee jerked her chin toward the Specter, standing beside Abigail like an evil mirror image. "The stories people in town tell about you—we know they're not true now! We know you, the *real* you!"

"Quiet!" the Specter howled. It snapped its fingers.

A branch snaked around Bailee's throat. She gasped as it tightened, pressing against her windpipe. It pressed harder even as her fingers clawed at the branches. She couldn't breathe. She felt shadows creep in at the edges of her eyes, threatening to swallow her up.

"Stop! Stop it!" screamed Madison.

Abigail's eyes went wide with fear. Just as quickly as her strength had returned, it was snuffed out. She faded, flickering weakly in the moonlight.

The Specter laughed. It snapped its fingers again, and the branches choking Bailee dropped away.

Bailee gulped air.

"Relax! It's just a scare. It's just a game!" the Specter said. "You all won't even remember in the morning—not much of it, anyway." It turned to Abigail. "Forget all those sappy memories and forget these kids, Abby. You've spread yourself paper-thin for them tonight. You gave it your all, but now you've got nothing left. You should join me. Or you might just disappear. For good this time."

Abigail backed away. She clapped her hands over her ears and squeezed her eyes shut. "No, no . . ."

The Specter advanced, towering over the ghost girl, a bright green flame against Abigail's frail flicker. It reached for her, mottled fingers grasping. "Last chance. What do you say, Abby?"

Abigail looked at Bailee and the others. Then at the Specter.

She hung her head. Then she whispered something indistinct.

"What? Didn't quite hear you, Abby." The Specter held a hand up to one ear.

Abigail looked up at it, a grim smile etched on her face. "I said, my name is *Abigail*."

Then she plunged her hands into the earth, fingers sinking in deep. A shock wave radiated out from her hands, rippling through the woods.

Bailee felt the branches binding her arms and legs go limp. She dropped to the forest floor. Around her, one by one, roots slipped from her friends' wrists and ankles. They were free.

Abigail collapsed.

CHAPTER 25
A TALE OF SHADOWS

Bailee knew she needed to run, but she felt rooted in place. She stared at Abigail, lying lifeless on the ground. The girl was barely visible now, only a faint shimmer.

Madison, Fen, Noah, and Carmen ran to Abigail's side.

"We've got her. Run!" Madison instructed.

Bailee tore her eyes from Abigail to meet Madison's gaze. She nodded once, then took off.

Behind her a screech of fury made the trees quiver and shake. The Specter blazed, brighter than ever before, washing the whole clearing in eerie green light. Bailee's shadow stretched out long and thin in front of her as if leading the way, guiding her to the bell.

Then, in a burst of smoke, the Specter appeared in front of her.

Bailee skidded to a halt, shielding her eyes against the Specter's glare. It loomed over her, its Abigail-like face contorted with rage.

"I . . . am getting . . . very . . . *very* . . . tired of this," the Specter panted. It staggered, unsteady on its feet, as if these last efforts had come at a great cost. Even the Specter's power appeared to have limits.

"Looks like you're running out of steam," Bailee said coldly. "If you'd been a little quicker, you could have stolen my journal. But the river got to it first."

"Yes, pity about that," said the Specter, wheezing. "There were some good stories in there. But I know you have more stored in that little brain of yours. And without an item to sacrifice, I can take as many as I please. Let's see, which one should I start with?"

The Specter dissolved into smoke. In a flash, Bailee's Wailing Widow stood before her, just as tragic and pale as she had been earlier. Then the Specter shifted again, and a zombie stood before Bailee. It staggered forward, all rotting flesh and puckered wounds. An eyeball hung from one socket, and maggots wriggled in its mouth.

Bailee felt her stomach lurch. Over the zombie's rotting shoulder, she could see the bell, so close, but still so far away.

"C'mon, I thought you liked scary stories." The Specter's zombie face grinned, forcing teeth to tumble out.

"I do. I just don't like what you do with them," Bailee spat.

"What?" The Specter put a hand to its chest in mock offense. "Isn't this what you wanted? To live out your very own Bellwoods tale? Look around—you're in the story now, Bailee. And it's all thanks to me. I bring your stories to life. I give your stories power! I make them true."

Bailee opened her mouth to reply, then paused. She scrunched up her nose. "No, you don't. Stories—they're already powerful on their own. You snatch up the ones that make us feel small and lonely and afraid. You twist the stories around, turning regular bats, wolves, and spiders into monsters. You take our stories and use them against us. You might make them look real. But that doesn't make them true. What you do—it's all just pretend." Bailee waved a dismissive hand. "You don't give them power. It's the other way around. You'd be nothing without our stories."

The Specter narrowed its eyes at her. "Maybe." It gave a low, dangerous growl. "Tell me, Bailee, how powerful is this story?"

The Specter turned to smoke. Then it re-formed.

Bailee drew back in horror.

A ghastly version of her grandmother stood before her with green, glowing skin. "What—what? Where

260

am I?" the fake Nan said, looking around the clearing, wide-eyed and confused. "I feel . . ." The rest of the words came out slow and slurred. One side of Nan's face fell, creating a lopsided look. The Specter's version of Nan staggered toward Bailee, then stumbled and fell.

Bailee's hands were trembling fists. "Leave my nan alone!" Hot tears splashed down her cheeks. The Specter shrieked with glee. It was toying with her; she knew that. She had to stay focused. She had to think.

"Yes, losing someone you love, that's the most terrifying tale of all." The Specter transformed back into its evil Abigail form again. "But don't worry, Bailee. Like you said, it's just a *story*. Your real nan is safe and sound, for now. But no one will be safe when I come to town. Unless . . ."

"Unless—what?" said Bailee, wiping furiously at her tears.

"Maybe we could work out some sort of deal. I've made deals before, you know. That's how the game got its rules. We could make a new deal right now."

"What sort of deal?" Bailee said cautiously.

"Let me win the game, and I promise to leave your nan alone when I come to town. What do you say?" The Specter reached out its hand.

"Don't do it, Bailee!" Madison yelled.

"Yeah, we can still win this thing," said Noah.

"Quiet!" The Specter blazed. With a flick of its hand, it picked up one of the fallen trees and hurled it at Bailee's friends. They dropped to the ground, letting the tree sail over their heads.

"That the best you got?" Fen shouted, standing up again, brushing dirt from his knees.

"I bet a Ceratosaurus could throw better than that!" Carmen yelled, popping up next to Fen. "They had very small arms," she added quickly.

The Specter ignored them. "Come on, Bailee. I don't offer deals like this to everyone. I can see into that mind of yours; your nan is not well. She might not survive an encounter with me. But if you take my deal, she's safe. Pinkie-swear." The Specter held out a hand again, extending its smallest finger.

Bailee scrambled away. She looked to her friends. Their voices were a jumble, urging her to refuse the Specter's deal and keep running. Then Bailee's eyes found Abigail, lying prone on the forest floor beside them. She was just a pale wisp now, barely discernible in the glare of the Specter's harsh light. Would she return next year? Would she be okay? Or was she lost forever?

Bailee felt resolve spark inside her. The Specter was right—partly, anyway. It was time to end the game. Not just tonight, but for good. But how? She urged herself to think. Something the Specter said had caught in her mind, turning over again and again like a leaf in the spoke of a bike wheel. It was the part about making stories true. The Specter's power was using their own imaginations against them. She wondered, what did the Specter fear? Maybe there was a way she could find out.

"You're right," Bailee said finally, letting her shoulders slump. "I can't run anymore. . . . I'll give you a story."

"Bailee! What are you doing?" Fen ran toward her. Madison, Carmen, and Noah followed. The Specter held up a hand, and they all stopped short, as if bumping up against an invisible wall.

"Bailee, you don't have to give up. We can keep going!" called Noah.

"Abigail would want us to keep trying!" Carmen agreed.

"Bailee, I know you're tired," said Madison. "But we can do this! We just need to—"

"No!" said Bailee, voice harsh. Her friends fell silent. "This needs to end. Now."

The Specter glowed brightly with glee. It reached for Bailee, fingers twitching, reaching, stretching, eager to snatch her story away.

"But I do have one condition." She held up a finger. "I won't let you *take* my story. I want to *tell* it to you instead."

The Specter paused. Its glittering eyes studied her.

Bailee knew it was sensing her thoughts, poking and prodding, itching to snatch up her story before she was ready. She willed her mind to clear. She conjured an image of a cool, clear night and imagined all her thoughts as distant, sparkling stars dotting the endless sky above, far from the Specter's reach.

"Your request is . . . highly unusual. Not part of the rules at all," said the Specter after a moment. It tried to sound disinterested, but excitement bubbled at the edges of its voice. The Specter liked the idea. This is what it had been asking for the whole game, wasn't it? For someone to tell it a story?

"But you can make an exception, can't you?" Bailee pressed. "We could make a deal."

The Specter put a long green finger to its lips, considering.

"Don't do it, Bailee!" Fen shouted.

"We can't give up!" Madison cried.

Bailee ignored them. She kept her eyes on the Specter. "C'mon, you're not up for another chase. You're fading fast, just like Abigail. It's been a long, hard game, and whatever power you have, it's nearly all used up." Bailee didn't know if this was true, but the Specter's expression hardened as she spoke. She had guessed right.

The Specter's face was a blank mask, but its green eyes glittered hungrily. "I suppose an amendment to the rules could be made. . . ." It waved an impatient hand. "Yes! Yes, we have a deal. Do it! Tell me your story!"

Bailee's heart skipped in her chest. On the other side of the clearing, she heard her friends groan.

This had better work, she thought.

Bailee closed her eyes and composed her face, keeping it blank. She couldn't give anything away, not until she was ready. Then she took a deep breath and began.

"There once was a girl who loved stories. The spookier, the better. Her favorite ones told the tale of a vengeful ghost haunting the woods around her little town. They also told of a game. And one day the girl and her friends agreed to play."

The Specter's eyes glittered again.

"They went deep into the woods and discovered a place where scary stories could come true. In a way . . . ," Bailee continued. "You see, during the game, the forest transformed. It became home to horrifying bats, a monstrous wolf, and other terrors. And, like the old stories said, a ghost did indeed walk the woods. But it wasn't the ghost these kids came to fear. They discovered something else haunting the woods, something far more frightening and strange—an apparition. It disguised itself as their worst nightmares and scariest stories. The game, it turned out, was just a ruse. An excuse to lure the children into the woods so the apparition could hunt them down, stealing their stories to add to its own collection of terrors."

The Specter glowed, recognizing itself in the story.

Good, thought Bailee. She went on, words picking up steam.

"One by one, the girl watched her friends fall prey to the apparition. Then it was her turn. She stood before it, the last remaining player in its terrible game. All looked lost. But then . . ."

". . . Then?" the Specter growled hungrily.

Bailee paused, stretching out the quiet until the Specter leaned in close. "A rustling came from the woods."

As if on cue, the sound of rustling leaves came from their right. Bailee felt her heartbeat quicken.

It was working.

The Specter started. "What was that?"

Bailee shrugged. "The girl didn't know. But she could feel the—*whatever it was*—watching her and the apparition. She could sense it *staring* at them. Shivers zipped up the girl's spine, and goose bumps crawled up her arms. She knew the apparition felt the same."

Bailee felt a shiver go through her, and her arms prickled. She watched as the Specter twitched. It gave a strange full-body shake and rubbed nervously at its arms as if suddenly chilled. "What? What's happening?" The Specter's face was a mixture of confusion and unease.

"The girl should have been afraid. After all, she'd spent the night running from her own most frightful stories come to life. But this time the girl had nothing to fear. Because she knew whatever was lurking in the shadows wouldn't harm her."

The rustling sounded again.

"Why? What is that? *What are you doing?*" The Specter's face screwed up into a menacing scowl. But Bailee saw the worry in its eyes now. It stormed over to the edge of the clearing, blazing brighter than ever before, sending strange-shaped shadows in every direction. It searched the woods, looking for the source of the sound.

"The apparition didn't know what was watching from the shadows," Bailee continued in a rush, "but it wondered what it could be. It began to imagine, thinking of terrible, terrifying things. After all, the apparition was a collector of scary stories; it had collected many during its time in the woods. It thought it knew what fear was. But only now did it begin to *feel* it. Especially after what happened next."

Harsh, unearthly laughter filled the woods.

The Specter flinched away from the sound. It whirled around to face Bailee. "No! I'm not afraid. I'm not! I AM fear. I AM your stories. You're the one who's supposed to be afraid, not me!" the Specter shouted.

"The apparition denied its terror!" Bailee yelled over the Specter's bluster. "But no one believed it, not even the apparition itself. Because at that moment its worst fear stepped out of the woods—one who could put an end to its game. For good."

A figure emerged from the woods then.

The sight made the Specter cry out in fury and Bailee gasp in shock.

A shadow stood before them.

It was person-shaped, just a moving patch of darkness. It made for a strange sight. But there was something familiar about the shade standing before them. Bailee looked down at her feet and realized she was missing something. Where once a shadow had stretched out behind her, there was now nothing. It was *her* shadow, moving around all on its own.

"No," the Specter said, realization and dread filling its voice. "No. NO!"

Bailee rolled with this unexpected development. "The girl had realized she couldn't win the game. Not as she was. Only part of her could escape the apparition's grasp—the girl's shadow. And it knew just what to do," she said with a grin. Her story had taken on a life of its own, just like she'd needed it to.

At this, Bailee's shadow took off. It bolted across the clearing, straight for the bell.

The Specter howled with fury. It dashed after the living silhouette, but its green glow only hastened the shadow on. The Specter reached for the shadow, its flailing arms passing right through.

"The apparition chased, but it had become a creature of light; it couldn't touch the girl's shadow," said Bailee, words coming fast. "The shadow girl ran for the old bell; nothing could stop it!" she called over the Specter's furious, exasperated roar.

Bailee's shadow drew up beside the bell. It glowed in the

Specter's harsh, green light, and a long, perfectly bell-shaped patch of darkness stretched out behind it. Bailee's shadow extended an arm toward the bell, reaching not for the rope hanging from it, but for the rope's shadow. For a split-second, the shade turned and looked at Bailee. Her shadow had no facial features, but Bailee imagined it smiling at her. She smiled back.

"And with one pull, the game was finished," Bailee whispered.

A sound echoed through the woods.

CLANG.

CHAPTER 26
THE GHOST'S GIFT

The sound of the bell filled the woods. Bailee almost fainted from relief. She heard her friends cheering wildly behind her. She turned, ready to run to them. But, suddenly, a thick fog took hold of the woods, blocking them from view. It surrounded Bailee, obscuring everything around her. It was if she'd walked into a misty cloud. The sound of her friends faded. Soon, it was as if the forest had ceased to exist. Bailee was alone in the fog.

"Hello?" she called. She moved forward, arms outstretched, reaching for trees, her friends, her shadow—anything.

"Not fair!" said a small voice, a high-pitched, bitter pout. "You cheated! That's not how the game's supposed to work!"

"What?" Bailee moved toward the sound.

A figure stepped out of the fog in front of her.

It was a little girl. A stained, old-fashioned dress hung from bone-thin shoulders. A cloud of blond, almost-white hair framed a sharp, pale face. Large, hollow eyes blazed at Bailee, glowing green.

It was the Specter.

"Your story was supposed to be for *me*! But you used it to win instead. You and the other one." The Specter stomped a foot.

"The other—who?"

Another figure stepped out of the fog behind the Specter. Bailee's shadow.

It was a perfect double of Bailee except it had no features, just a flat, dark shape. It crossed its arms at the Specter and tapped an impatient foot.

Bailee shook her head in disbelief at the sight. This was the weirdest night of her entire life. Hands down.

The Specter addressed the shadow. "Well, then. What do you want?"

The shadow gestured. It appeared to be speaking, but

Bailee couldn't make out the words. Maybe she didn't speak shadow.

But, evidently, the Specter did. Its green eyes flashed, and its pale face scrunched with rage. "No. No way!"

The shadow gestured again.

"No!" shouted the Specter. "If you take it, I won't be able to play again! That's not fair!"

Bailee looked from the Specter to her shadow. If looks could kill, Bailee's shadow would have been toast.

After a moment the Specter-girl slumped. "Fine. But I'm not finished, you'll see."

The shadow's head bobbed as if things had been settled. Then it turned and walked into the fog. The gray mist parted like a curtain. It pulled back to reveal the bell. It sat amid a scrubby patch of grass, looking absurdly normal after a night of such strange terrors.

The shadow walked up to the bell, then turned to face Bailee and the Specter. It waved. Then it reached out and put a hand to the bell.

Bailee's mouth dropped.

The bell transformed under the shadow's touch. It began to flatten and dim as if all the light had been sucked out of it. Soon it was nothing more than a shadow itself, a bell-shaped silhouette. The swirling fog crept in again, swallowing up the bell and Bailee's shadow.

Bailee found herself alone with the Specter.

"Your turn now," grumped the Specter, turning to her. "What do *you* want?"

"Why—why do you look like this?"

"Why do you think? It's another one of my stories." The Specter did a grim little twirl. "Do you like it? It was my first one." It plucked at the dress and smiled up at Bailee, eyes glittering.

"Your *first* story?" Bailee said, perplexed.

The Specter nodded. "I got it a long, long time ago. There were these kids, ones just like you. They used to gather around the bell to tell scary tales. They were fans of the old superstitions, you see. About the so-called spirits in the woods. They

would ring the bell before the stories began to summon spirits forth. Then, when the stories were done, they'd ring it again to send them away. They thought it was good fun. But they never *really* expected to encounter me."

"You're a *spirit*?" said Bailee, eyebrows raised.

The Specter shrugged. "Depends on your definition, I guess. These woods are a special place, you see. It's easy for those like me to come and go here—well, easier. And something about the stories those kids told called to me. Every time I heard the bell, I came to listen. They couldn't see me, of course. No one can see me, not without my disguises. I was their silent, invisible audience. It was such good fun . . . except, after they were done, they'd ring the bell and send me away again. I never liked that part." The Specter's eyes grew cold and hard.

Bailee frowned, struck by a reluctant jab of sympathy for the Specter. It had spoken of being lonely when it had tried to win over Abigail. At the time, Bailee thought perhaps it was just another trick. But maybe it hadn't been.

"I didn't want to be sent away. I wanted more stories! Then, one Halloween night, I got what I wanted. The kids had gathered in the woods for another spine-tingling tale. The storyteller, a girl not unlike yourself, told one about a child possessed by a demonic spirit." The Specter's grin went wide and wolfish. "It was a frightfully fun story. But that wasn't the only thing that caught my interest that night. That night, the storyteller wore a beautiful clip in her hair. I remember thinking it was so pretty, the way it glittered in the moonlight. I reached out for it, wanting to hold it. I didn't think I'd be able to touch it, not really. I'd never been able to grasp things from the living world. But somehow, this time, I did.

Maybe it was because the boundaries between my world and yours are particularly thin on Halloween. Or maybe it's just another of the forest's mysteries. Whatever the reason, I reached out and stole that clip from her. And when I held it in my hand, I realized I had taken something else, too."

Bailee could guess what it was.

"I felt her story pulsing inside. The clip was more than just a pretty thing; it let me keep her story! Holding it made me feel strange. But powerful . . ." A dreamy, faraway sort of look washed over the Specter's face. "Then suddenly the kids screamed. They all jumped up and ran away. No one looked back. I was confused at first. Then I looked down and realized, they could see me! Well, they saw a child possessed by a demon standing in front of them, the *same* child possessed by a demon from the story they'd just heard. Not only had I stolen the story when I took the girl's hair clip, but I had also *become* it. What a fright that must have been!" The Specter doubled over with laughter.

Bailee shuddered.

"At first I was mad the kids went away. But then I realized they forgot to ring the bell. They forgot to send me away! I hoped the kids would come back and tell more stories. I waited and waited. But they didn't come." The Specter's face hardened. "So I decided I'd go find some stories for myself. I left the woods and went into the little town nearby. I found lots of stories there, and with them I grew strong. But, alas, the little town suffered because of it." The Specter shrugged, looking like this was something that couldn't be helped.

"Troubled times," whispered Bailee. But the Specter went on.

"After a while some of the kids who'd been in the woods that Halloween night remembered about the bell. They didn't know for sure that I was the reason bad things were happening in town, but they thought, just maybe, ringing the bell would put things right again. They gathered their courage and returned to the woods. But I was waiting for them—with a deal in mind."

"Of course," said Bailee.

"I proposed a game of sorts. If they could beat me to the bell, I'd return to my world and leave everyone in peace for one whole year. But if I tagged them before they could reach it, I was free to roam the town. I'd seen kids playing a game just like it in the woods plenty of times. This time I wanted them to play it with me."

"And the Bellwoods Game was born," Bailee finished.

"Exactly. More rules followed in time. All good games change over the years, just like a good story does. And, of course, I employed a very different strategy after Abigail joined me here in the woods." The Specter-girl grinned. "There were so many stories about her after she fell into that river. She was the perfect disguise! Kids were so busy being afraid of Abigail, they never even considered something worse was hunting them. It was all terribly funny." The Specter sighed dreamily. Then its expression went hard. "But then that shadow of yours came along, stole my bell, and *ruined everything*!" The Specter stomped and kicked.

Bailee said nothing, just watched until the Specter's temper tantrum subsided.

"Go on, then," it said, finally collecting itself. "What do you want? That shadow took its gift, and now it's time for yours, since *technically* you both won. And hurry up, I'm tired now." The little girl stretched and yawned, like a grumpy kid awake long past her bedtime.

This was it, Bailee realized. The Ghost's Gift.

Her mind reeled. After all that had happened tonight, she had completely forgotten about this part of the game. She thought about everything she'd struggled with the past three weeks—Nan's health; her overworked, absent parents; the distance between Madison and her; and the look in Fen's eyes when he had said their friendship was over. She'd felt so alone, like everything around her was slipping away. Now standing in front of her was her chance to make things go back to the way they used to be.

Bailee opened her mouth to tell the Specter what she wanted. But something stopped her.

Abigail.

Bailee sighed. The past few weeks had been hard for her and her family, but they were nothing compared to what Abigail had been through all these years alone in the woods. She'd given up so much to help the kids of Fall Hollow and to keep the town safe. She'd spent years roaming the woods, looking for peace and never finding it.

Bailee knew what she had to do.

"I want Abigail's memories back," she said to the Specter finally.

The Specter raised an eyebrow. "Why?"

"Because," said Bailee, "they belong to her, not you. She should have them. She should remember who she was. Who she *is*."

The Specter rolled its eyes. "That is like, the worst request I've ever gotten. But fine. Here." It reached out and grabbed hold of Bailee's hand.

Bailee instinctively flinched. The Specter-girl's hand was as cold as ice. But soon Bailee felt her own fingers grow warm. She felt a rushing feeling in her fingertips. Then a swirl of unfamiliar thoughts flooded her mind—Abigail's memories.

"There. That's all her memories. You'll have to carry them around until you find something to hold them. It's got to be the right something too. You can't just put them any old place," said the Specter quickly, as if this was all very obvious. It was yawning now. It stretched a final time, then turned and walked into the fog.

"Wait!" cried Bailee, running after it. "What do you mean? What's the *right* something?"

The Specter ignored her. "Oh! And you should know that by accepting your Ghost's Gift, you agree not to tell anyone what happened here tonight. Sorry, should have mentioned that earlier. It's another rule. Hope you don't mind!" it called back at her, only a silhouette against the fog now. "But if you think the game's over, you're wrong. I always find a way to play. You'll see."

Then the Specter was gone.

"Wait!" Bailee tried to chase after the Specter. But her head suddenly felt light and dizzy. She fell to her hands and knees.

Her world went dark.

When she opened her eyes again, she found herself at the edge of the woods. She was back at the cemetery. They all were—Noah, Carmen, Madison, and Fen. They were sprawled in the grass beside her, moaning as if waking from a much too short nap. Bailee felt dew soaking the knees of her jeans. That's when she realized the rest of her clothes were dry, like she'd never fallen in the river. She looked at her hands, no longer scratched and dirty from stumbling around in the woods all night. Bailee pushed herself to her feet. In the moonlight she could see her shadow hovering beneath her, back where it belonged.

It was as if the Bellwoods Game had never happened.

She stood up, unsteady on her feet. Her classmates pressed in around them, shouting questions. Their voices were an unintelligible tangle.

"How? What—" Fen murmured next to Bailee. She went to him, extending a hand.

Beside them, Madison and Carmen were rubbing their eyes as if waking up. Someone must have given Noah a pen because he was already sitting up, unsteadily jotting down notes. They look dazed. But fine.

They had made it out of the woods. They were safe.

They had won the game.

CHAPTER 27
BEYOND THE WOODS

It'd been easy to avoid questions about where Bailee had been Halloween night. When she returned home, her mom was still at work, and Nan was asleep on her favorite chair in front of the woodstove. Magic purred in her lap. Bailee draped a blanket over them, grateful to find Nan safe and sound. Bailee climbed the stairs to her room and collapsed into bed, still wearing her clothes.

By the time she trudged down to breakfast the next morning, stiff and unrested, the Bellwoods Game felt like a strange, distant dream. Her memories felt too impossible to be real. But just when she'd almost convinced herself they couldn't have happened, she felt a sharp pain in her temple.

Abigail's memories were there, pulsing alongside her own,

bursting to get out. The game had definitely happened. Even if it was technically over, Bailee still wasn't done with Abigail Snook.

When she rolled up to school on her bike, she found kids standing around in groups, shivering, with hoods pulled up against the early November chill. Leaves rattled in the gutter, and wind tugged at Bailee's jacket as she knelt to lock up her bike. She saw heads swivel in her direction, noticing her arrival. She hurried toward school, pretending not to feel the heat of their stares. She was used to curious looks now, ever since the dare. But today the whispers following in her wake were different. Because she wasn't the girl who'd gotten her whole class detention and her friend suspended anymore. Today she was the newest Bellwoods Game winner.

"I swear I heard a wolf howl come from the woods. Do you think she saw it?" came a whisper to Bailee's left.

"I heard the creepiest laugh," said another. "Like, seriously spooky. I never believed in the stuff people said about the woods before. But now . . ."

"I walk through the woods on my way to school every day," someone else said. "I didn't see any wolves or ghosts, but—get this—the bell is *gone*. Vanished!"

This caught Bailee's attention. Just about everything had gone back to normal after the bell rang—her cuts disappeared; her river-soaked clothes had dried. But if this rumor was true, the bell was gone for good.

Bailee craned her neck to locate the source of the whisper. Then she smacked into someone.

"Oh! I'm sorry!" Bailee held her hands up apologetically.

"Psh, not likely," came the sneering reply. It was Gabby.

Bailee groaned. Of all the people she could have run into.

Gabby turned back to her conversation with Riley and Tate, pretending Bailee wasn't there. But Tate stepped in front of Bailee, face eager. "What was it like playing the game? Did you *really* see the ghost?"

Bailee started to reply. But the moment her brain conjured Abigail's image, she felt a pressure in her throat. It was like an invisible hand had clamped down on her windpipe, ready to squeeze it shut. She coughed. "I . . . I really can't say," she squeaked out. Then she hurried off, making for the school doors.

"Forget her." Gabby's voice followed Bailee up the front steps. "She'd probably just lie about what happened last night anyway."

Bailee sighed. No matter what she did, Gabby was determined to hate her. Even if she *had* wanted to tell Tate what had happened during the game, the Specter's rules wouldn't let her. She felt a pressure in her throat again. She understood Arlo's coughing fits before the game.

Then, as if summoned by her thoughts, Arlo was there.

They jogged up the school steps toward her. "I was hoping I'd catch you before class. Just wanted to congratulate you on—" Arlo coughed and put a hand to their throat. "Well . . . you know." They nodded toward the Bellwoods.

"Oh. Thanks," Bailee said, feeling a little proud.

"I also wanted to say I'm . . . I'm sorry." Arlo looked at the ground now. "I tried to . . . I wish I could have—"

"It's okay." Bailee waved Arlo's apology away. "You tried to warn us. I get how difficult it is to—" It was her turn to cough now. She winced, rubbing at her throat. "Wow, that's not a pleasant feeling."

"You never get used to it," Arlo said, face grim. They sighed. "I just wanted to make sure you and the other players are okay."

"I'll probably lay off the horror novels. But only for the next week or two." Bailee managed a grin. "But yeah, I'm fine. The others are too. I think." She hoped this was true.

Arlo let out a slow breath. "Good." The two of them stood together for a moment, neither knowing quite what to say. Someone called Arlo's name. "I guess I should go. Just wanted to . . . you know—" Arlo coughed again. "Well, let's just say that everyone in Fall Hollow owes you a thank-you. Even if they don't realize it." They gave her another nod, then turned to leave.

"It's over now," Bailee called after Arlo's retreating figure. "For good this time. At least, I think so. No one else should ever have to—" Her memory of her shadow stealing away the bell made her throat squeeze shut again. "You know what I mean," she wheezed, tilting her head toward the woods.

Arlo stopped, turning to the Bellwoods. They shivered, but not because of the November chill. "Good," they said. They gave Bailee a final nod, then joined a group of friends chatting by the basketball court.

Bailee smiled to herself as she pushed through the front doors of school. Not being able to speak about playing the Bellwoods Game was going to be tough. But knowing there was someone out there who understood made her feel a little lighter.

She walked the halls of Beckett Elementary. Eyes followed her. So did whispers. She ignored them. She'd hoped winning the Bellwoods Game would put an end to the gossip. But it looked like she'd only given them something different to whisper about.

She opened her locker and started piling books inside. She looked up just in time to catch Fen coming down the hallway toward her, Brendan and Luca in tow. Bailee smiled and raised a hand. But Fen frowned and looked away. Like she didn't exist.

Bailee's face fell. What had she expected? Only the Bellwoods Game winner remembered their time in the woods. Everyone else forgot. If Fen didn't remember the game, he wouldn't remember Madison's confession either. As far as he knew, none of it had even happened.

Bailee unloaded more books into her locker. Her throat tightened, but not because of the Specter's rules this time. As horrible as last night had been, her friends had been there for her. They'd come together. But now none of them would remember. And thanks to the Specter's rules, she couldn't even remind them.

The first bell rang. Bailee slammed her locker shut and hurried to class, blinking away tears. She'd hoped playing the Bellwoods Game would fix everything. But now she felt more alone than ever.

Bailee kept to herself all day, just like she usually did. A few times, kids got up the courage to ask her about the game. But she ignored them. Even if she could have told them what had happened, she didn't feel like talking.

She watched her friends throughout the day. None of them

looked much interested in talking about the game either. Madison and Fen, used to being at the center of swirling activity at Beckett, were unusually subdued. They dodged questions and avoided the gossiping crowds. Their eyes were rimmed with dark circles, their expressions both wary and worn. Noah and Carmen, unprepared for their newfound popularity, hurried through the day looking just as exhausted as Madison and Fen but more flustered. News had spread about Noah's unexpected participation in the game. Kids who'd been referring to him as New Kid for the past two months started greeting him by name, then grilled him for Bellwoods Game info. At lunch a popular eighth-grade girl sat down in the chair next to Carmen to ask if she'd really fought off Abigail Snook single-handedly with her flashlight, like the rumors said. Carmen had been so shocked by the girl's interest in her that she dropped her sandwich on the floor.

Kids had lots of questions for the Bellwoods Game players. But no matter who they asked, the answer that Fen, Madison, Carmen, and Noah gave was always the same—*I don't know.* They repeated the phrase all day long. And, for them, it was the truth.

But no one believed them.

By the time the last bell of the day had rung, Bailee had heard enough about the Bellwoods. Her head was throbbing. Abigail's memories pulsed restlessly amid her own, a constant reminder of all she couldn't share with her friends. She slammed her locker shut, grateful to go home and not be constantly reminded about the game for a while.

Then Noah appeared at her elbow. Fen, Madison, and Carmen were with him, looking both confused and expectant.

"We need to talk," Noah said. He held his notepad out to her, the one he'd carried with him during the game. It was open to a page with just one hasty scrawl, one he must have managed to capture before the Specter stole his pen.

The winner knows *what happened.*

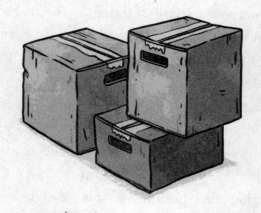

CHAPTER 28
LOST AND FOUND

"**Y**our friends are here!" Bailee's mom called from downstairs.

"Coming!" Bailee heaved a box onto a pile of others, then brushed her hands together, sending clouds of dust into the air.

It'd been two weeks since she'd played the Bellwoods Game. She and her family were at Nan's house, packing. The house had sold, and everything had to be moved out.

"Don't carry those boxes down by yourself," her mom called. "I'm sending your father up."

"But I'm so strong." Bailee flexed an arm.

"Oh, we know that." Her dad started up the stairs. "But I have to make myself useful somehow."

"We had him wrapping breakables," said Nan as she passed

through the downstairs hall carrying a pair of candlesticks. "But he was not suited to the position."

"When you're clumsy, they give you less to do." Bailee's dad winked.

He'd arrived home last night. He'd come with good news. The company he'd been working for had offered him a full-time position, one that would allow him to work remotely most of the time. He was home for good.

Bailee laughed, then bounded past her dad down the stairs. She stepped out the front door into thin sunlight.

"Hope everyone's ready to carry some boxes!" Bailee waved at Madison, Fen, and Carmen as she watched them drop their bikes on the grass and walk up to the house.

"Madison said I had to come," grumbled Fen with a smile. Madison rolled her eyes.

"Noah's still coming too, right?" Carmen asked.

"He said he might be late. He had to talk to Chivers after class," Bailee said.

"Uh-oh," Fen said, making a face.

Madison snorted. "Students can talk one-on-one with teachers without being in trouble, you know."

"News to me," Fen replied.

"I'm here!" Noah shouted as he biked up the driveway toward them, out of breath.

"Chivers give you the go-ahead?" Bailee asked as he raced up the porch steps.

He gave her two thumbs up. "Beckett's first-ever student paper is a go."

Everyone clapped.

"Thanks." Noah practically bounced with excitement. "We're still figuring out a lot of the details, but we're hoping to use the story I'm writing about Abigail as our first feature. Chivers even offered to put me in touch with someone who knew Abigail a long time ago."

"Are you going to tell this person that you *also* know Abigail?" Carmen asked, grinning.

"Uh, I figured I might leave out any mention of ghosts."

"Smart." Fen nodded.

"Now all we have to do is recruit more students to work on the paper." Noah eyed his friends.

Madison's eyes lit up. "Can there be a theater review section?"

"Does the paper need a photographer? My dad got me a DSLR for my last birthday. I'd love an excuse to use it more," Carmen added.

"Yeah, absolutely!" Noah bobbed his head at both of them.

"Does your paper publish fiction? I think I finally figured out a new ending to the Wailing Widow," Bailee said.

"Great idea!" Noah beamed.

"Count me in too, then," Fen said.

Everyone looked at him.

"Really?" Bailee raised an eyebrow.

"Hey, you know I'm always up for trying new things."

"Actually, that is true. To a fault, even," Madison agreed.

"That's right! I'm up for anything. Except maybe . . . you know." He shivered, nodding toward the Bellwoods across the street.

Thanks to Noah's meticulous notes, taken before the Specter stole his pen, Bailee's friends had managed to piece together much of what had happened during the game. Bailee helped as much as she could, choking and spluttering in the process. It'd been slow going at first, but each memory jarred loose another. Then another. Soon all the memories had come flooding back. Even the ones they could have done without. Noah wasn't happy about remembering the spiders.

There was only one thing Bailee's friends didn't know. Something she finally felt able to share—where she'd really disappeared to during the Day of the Dare.

"I'm so sorry," Noah had said after Bailee finished telling them about Nan's TIA.

Carmen gave her a tight hug.

"I'm so glad Nan's okay," said Madison, blinking back tears.

"Me too," said Fen.

It'd been a tough conversation, but Bailee went home feeling lighter that day. Her worries weren't gone. But the weight of them felt easier to carry now that she had friends to help her.

Things had gone back to normal after that. Well, as normal as possible, considering what they now knew about the Bellwoods. None of them slept well in the weeks following the game. They had recurring nightmares about the Bellwoods and everything they'd seen during the game. They spent their days trying to keep busy, grateful for regular kid stuff like homework and hanging out with friends. Helping Nan move was just the sort of distraction they all needed.

"Thanks so much for coming, everyone!" said Nan, appearing on the porch behind Bailee. "You're all staying for dinner, correct? There's enough chili back at Bailee's house to feed the entire town."

There were enthusiastic nods all around.

"Excellent! I've got jobs for everyone, but first—Bailee, can I steal you away for a moment?" Nan asked.

Bailee nodded. She left her friends and followed Nan inside.

She spied a small rectangular gift sitting on the stairs.

"What's that?" Bailee asked.

"Better open it and find out," said Nan, eyes crinkling in the corners.

Bailee picked up the gift and tore off its brightly colored wrapping paper. Inside, Bailee found a brand-new journal.

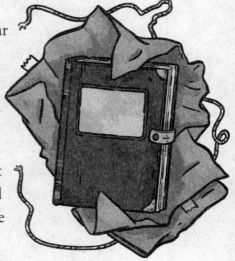

"Nan, this is great! Thank you!" Bailee wrapped her arms around her grandmother.

Nan hugged back. "I noticed you haven't been writing much lately. I thought maybe you needed a fresh journal for writing new stories."

Bailee grinned. "You always know just what I need."

Then, a quick burst of pain in her head made her wince. She put a hand to her temple, feeling Abigail's memories pushing restlessly against her fingertips. Bailee needed extra space for her own thoughts more than ever these days.

"Bailee?" Her mom's voice came from the kitchen. "You all done packing up Margery's room?"

"Uh, yeah. I'll double-check." She gave Nan another quick hug. Then she bounded up the stairs and went to the room at the end of the hall.

Aunt Margery's old room looked smaller with all its contents packed away. A fine layer of dust carpeted the hardwood, stirred up from all the packing. The floral wallpaper was faded and starting to peel in one corner. Stacks of boxes littered the space full of Margery's old belongings from when she was a girl. She hadn't been interested in keeping anything. Maybe her fear of Fall Hollow ghosts extended to her old belongings, too? Bailee didn't know. Whatever the reason, they'd be donating the lot of it.

Bailee pulled open the closet door and peered inside to see if she'd missed anything. All looked clear.

Then something brushed against Bailee's leg.

"Goodness!" she cried. Magic was there. He sat between her feet, yellow eyes staring up at her. "Do you have to scare me every time?"

Magic meowed, then slipped inside the closet.

"Hey now." Bailee leaned in to scoop up the cat. Then she paused, watching.

He pawed at a corner. Then he turned and meowed at her again.

"Is something there?" Bailee slipped her phone out of her pocket and turned on the flashlight. She nudged Magic out of the way, searching.

One of the floorboards was sticking up. Bailee grabbed it and, with a wiggle, the board broke free from the rest. She inched farther into the closet, angling her phone so she could see into the small, dark hole the floorboard had left behind.

"Ugh, if there's a dead mouse in here . . ." She looked warily at Magic.

The cat meowed again.

Bailee grimaced as she stuck her hand in, expecting to find a rodent corpse. Instead her fingers felt something metallic. She pulled it out.

It was a silver locket.

At that moment, Bailee felt a strange rush of energy go through her. It started at her temples, then traveled down her

arm and through her fingertips. With it went all of Abigail's memories. They flowed into the locket.

"Whoa," said Bailee, feeling a little light-headed.

Magic rubbed against her arm, purring.

"What's that?" said Nan, appearing in the bedroom doorway behind them.

Bailee held up her find. "Was this Aunt Margery's?"

"I don't think so," said Nan, brows knitting together. "Never seen it before."

"I think I have," Bailee murmured.

Later, with packing and dinner finished, Bailee and her friends slipped out of her house and into the woods. They used their phones to light their way, jumping at every snap of a twig, certain the Specter was there. But no hungry spirits haunted the woods today.

They navigated to the clearing where the bell once stood. It was empty now. Like the bell never existed.

"Wild," said Noah, crouching to inspect. "If I hadn't seen the bell with my own eyes, I never would have believed it'd been here at all."

Bailee looked closer at the place it had once been. Was she seeing things? Or did she detect a slight bell-shaped shadow? She reached for it. But her fingers found nothing.

Wherever her own shadow had taken the bell, it was well out of reach.

"If it can't ring to begin the game, the game can't be played," said Carmen, nodding approvingly.

"The way you tricked the Specter into using its own power against itself—genius!" agreed Madison.

"I wish you could tell us what happened after!" Fen threw his hands up. "Come on. It had to have something to do with the Ghost's Gift, right? Tell me that part of the game was real."

Bailee gave him a wink.

"I'm taking that as a yes!" said Fen. "Which means . . . oh no." He clapped a hand to his forehead. "If I'd won, I really could have wished to be a pro basketball player!"

Madison clucked her tongue at him.

"But getting rid of the bell and ending the game forever was good too, obviously," he added hastily.

Bailee grinned. Her friends didn't know what had happened between the Specter and her after the bell had been rung. Or how her shadow had really been the one to spirit away the bell. But maybe she'd work out a way to tell them someday.

"No one should ever have to play that terrible game again," said Madison. From the back pocket of her jeans, she pulled out a small book, the one holding all the Bellwoods Game rules. She turned and walked to the bridge, pausing halfway across. She watched the Hollow River rushing below her. Then she tossed the book over the edge. It splashed into the water, and the strong current quickly pulled it under. She watched as it disappeared into the river's murky depths.

Bailee joined Madison. "You know, usually I don't condone littering, but I think that's the right spot for that particular notebook. A place where no one will ever find it," said Bailee.

Madison nodded. "Jade would lose it if she found out. When she picked me to be Keeper, she went on and on about how accepting the role meant I must pass on the rules to the next group of players. But then, maybe if Jade knew the whole story of the Bellwoods Game, she'd have felt differently."

Bailee put an arm around her friend's shoulders. They rejoined the others.

"Where do you think we should leave it?" Carmen asked.

"Maybe where the bell used to be?" suggested Noah.

Bailee nodded. She slipped something silver from the pocket of her jacket—the locket.

She placed it on a small mossy rock near where the bell once stood.

Bailee hadn't been able to fully explain how she'd come to find the locket and its significance. Or how Abigail's stolen memories now pulsed inside it. But when Bailee had shown them the locket and pointed to the woods, her friends had understood enough.

"Do you think she's still here? Even after everything that happened?" asked Fen.

They looked around, half expecting Abigail to appear. The woods around them were quiet and still.

"Wherever she is, I hope she finds peace," said Carmen. Everyone nodded.

They watched the locket for a moment, then turned to leave. The plan was to collect their bikes from Bailee's house, then head over to Noah's for a movie marathon. No scary ones, they'd decided, despite Bailee's protestations.

"All those times we spent talking about the game, I never thought it would be like this," said Madison with a shake of her head as they made their way out of the woods.

"I definitely wouldn't have played if I did," said Fen.

Bailee smirked. "Um, you totally would have."

Fen laughed. "Yeah. You're right."

"If there's one thing for certain, there's still a lot we don't know about the game," said Carmen.

"And the woods," Noah agreed. "I have a lot more research planned. You in, Carmen?"

"Absolutely. We can start researching tonight! Maybe we could even stop at the library tomorrow morning."

"Leave it to you two to make something as wild as what we just went through into a homework assignment," Fen groaned.

They came to the edge of the woods. Fen, Noah, and Carmen stepped out, laughing and debating movie choices. Bailee made to follow, then realized someone was missing.

Madison had stopped just inside the woods, phone in hand. She was staring at the screen, a strange expression on her face.

"What? What is it?" Bailee doubled back. She peeked at Madison's phone.

On the screen was a picture of a cartoon ghost, the same one that kids had been posting before the game. Bailee had almost forgotten about it. It glowed a glittering, sickly green on Madison's screen.

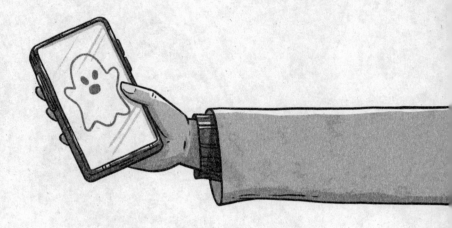

"What's happening?" Bailee asked.

"I don't know. It just . . . appeared."

They didn't say anything for a moment. The image glowed, then flickered, and then went blank. Madison's usual home screen reappeared, as if nothing had happened.

"What . . . ?" asked Madison, eyes wide.

Bailee shook her head, an uneasy feeling in her stomach.

"C'mon! Movie night!" shouted Fen, hands cupped to his mouth.

Madison tucked her phone away. She and Bailee hurried after their friends.

Bailee shot one last look over her shoulder at the Bellwoods.

Inside, bare branches creaked and rattled in the blustery wind. Shadows shifted, and a small, unseen creature rustled somewhere in the crisp leaves blanketing the ground. For a second Bailee thought she saw someone standing among the trees—a girl wearing a red cloak with a long braid draped over one shoulder. Something silver glinted at her collarbone. She smiled and waved.

Bailee blinked.

And the girl was gone.

ACKNOWLEDGMENTS

When I first started daydreaming about the story that would become *The Bellwoods Game*, I knew my characters would have to work together if they had any hope of winning in the end. The success of any adventure, whether in stories or real life, is rarely the work of one person but rather the collaborative effort of a great team. The same goes for creating books. *The Bellwoods Game* wouldn't exist without the combined talents of so many kind, hard-working, and supportive people.

To my incredible agent, Andrea Morrison, thank you for believing in this story and believing I could write it too. There's nothing I'd rather be doing than making books, and I'm so grateful I get to do it with you.

To my editor Alex Borbolla, thank you for taking a chance on this spooky tale. You understood the heart of this book right away, and your brilliant insight made this story shine so much brighter than I ever knew it could.

To my editor Kristie Choi, thank you for taking up the torch for this story, sharing my vision, and carrying us over the finish line (and for sending adorable cat pics). Having you in my corner has meant so much.

A big thank-you as well to Reka Simonsen for overseeing and guiding this project.

To designer and art director Lauren Rille, working with you is always such a joy. Thank you for your talent, creativity, enthusiasm, and for making this book look so beautiful.

Thank you to Jacquelynne Hudson-Underwood. Executing the design for the complicated interiors was a feat, and you are a champion.

Clare McGlade, thank you for lending your keen eyes and proofreading superpowers to this story.

Tatyana Rosalia, thank you for your expert organizational skills and for helping make *Bellwoods* more beautiful than I ever dreamed.

To all the hard-working folks at Atheneum Books for Young Readers and Simon & Schuster, thank you for making such special books for kids.

A big thank-you to Mom and Dad for filling my world with books, teaching me to dream big, and, of course, for all your love. Thank you to Jim and Kelly for your support over the years. I'm so lucky to have you both as family. Thank you to Emily for always cheering me on and being the best sister and friend anyone could ask for. Thank you as well to Ken and

Cathy for your constant love, encouragement, and for always offering to feed Jamie and I when we're tired and overworked.

Thank you as well to my many pals who've been an endless source of support and inspiration over the years. Shen, thank you for being an early reader and always being someone I can lean on. Anne, thank you for years of love and laughter and for helping my research process with our walks in the woods. To the talented Dungeon Delve crew: Jori, Diana, Rachel, and (horror genius and ultimate movie-recommender) Steve, thank you all for being early eyes on this project, for your encouragement, and for having my back during our adventures, both real and fantastical. Thank you to the Picture Book Pals (particularly Dorothy Leung for inviting me to be part of the group), it's been a privilege getting to know you all and share in your kidlit journeys.

A special thank-you to Jamie, my fiercest supporter, my best friend, my calm in every storm. There's no one I'd rather have beside me during this adventure. I know I can tackle anything with you by my side.

Lastly, thank you, dear reader, for braving the woods with me. A story only works when there's someone to share it with, and I'm so grateful to have been able to share this one with you.

...e must enter a chilling otherworld of ghosts, ...nes, and monsters to play a game with deadly ...nsequences in this delightfully eerie series.

★ "A fascinating and memorable world, and a brilliant protagonist."

—*Bulletin of the Center for Children's Books* on *The Nighthouse Keeper*, starred review